SARA'S PAST

Ernie Lindsey

Copyright © 2014 by Ernie Lindsey.

All rights reserved. No part of this publication may be reproduced, distributed or transmitted in any form or by any means, including photocopying, recording, or other electronic or mechanical methods, without the prior written permission of the publisher, except in the case of brief quotations embodied in critical reviews and certain other noncommercial uses permitted by copyright law.

Publisher's Note: This is a work of fiction. Names, characters, places, and incidents are a product of the author's imagination. Locales and public names are sometimes used for atmospheric purposes. Any resemblance to actual people, living or dead, or to businesses, companies, events, institutions, or locales is completely coincidental.

ISBN-13: 978-1494879334
ISBN-10: 1494879336

Sara's Past / Ernie Lindsey. -- 1st ed.

This is no game.

ONE

Detective Emerson Barker was *not* happy.

He marched across the playground, enduring yet another sprinkling, foggy afternoon in Portland, Oregon. You'd think the gods would allow the weekends to be nice, if nothing else, but at least the changing leaves gave some color to the drab, dreary gray.

As he approached the squealing children, he thought about his former partner, a memory that would never fade.

Detective Jonathan Johnson, DJ, JonJon, had taken a bullet trying to protect the woman that Barker now trudged toward. It had been honorable of DJ, trading his life for this small family, but damn, one life lost was one too many.

Barker thought, *It's been what, well over a year already? Time don't wait for the dead to come back, but we still miss you, cowboy.*

He stepped in a puddle, splashing sandy, dirty water onto his slacks, making his left shoe soggy and cold. "Son of a—" He caught the last word, wrenched it back, realizing he was within earshot of Sara

Winthrop and her children. The twins, Lacey and Callie, and Jacob, her son, who was unfortunate enough to have not one, but two older sisters to torment him.

Over the past year, Barker had occasionally checked in on the Winthrops, making sure they were mentally sound and had gotten their lives nudged in the right direction again. Surviving the kidnapping, beating that crazy girl, Shelley Sergeant, at her own game—it'd been rougher on Sara than the kids.

Although, since he'd last checked maybe two months ago, she seemed to be settling into something that could resemble normality. Finally.

Which is exactly why he was so red-faced pissed regarding his current assignment. But, as they say, bullshit rolls downhill, and he was left with the task of asking Sara Winthrop to come out of retirement, so to speak. As he approached Sara but before he greeted her, his last thought was of Donald Timms, the pristine jerk from the FBI, and how he wished he'd told the self-righteous dickwad where he could shove it back in the captain's office that morning.

***

Sara moved from child to child to child, pushing

them on the swings, laughing and avoiding the shoe-scuffed, rain-filled crevices below each one. "Watch your feet," she said. "The sharks might nibble on your toes."

The mist had evolved into a drizzle, and Barker angled his umbrella against the wind, blocking the cool shards of precipitation prickling his cheeks. He said, "You do know it's raining, right?"

Sara jumped, yelped, and covered her mouth. She said, "Barker. Jesus, you scared the sh—you scared the *crap* out of me."

Still jumpy, Barker thought. *That'll probably never go away. Not completely.*

"Sorry about that. I know better."

Sara forced an awkward smile and nodded. "You should."

"Went by your house. Miss Willow said I could find you down here." The wind kicked up and brought with it heavier, fatter drops of rain. Barker shuddered and turned his back to the onslaught. "Never stops, does it? Can we go over to that shelter? I'd like to talk to you about something."

"Sure. Kids? Come on, it's raining too much, let's follow Mr. Bloodhound over to the shelter, okay?" Like most Portland children who were used to it, the rain was just another aspect of typical northwestern weather to ignore, and they protested. Sara insisted and off they went, running, with the twins in the lead and Jacob quickly catching up.

Barker took a longer, steadier look at Sara. A few more streaks of gray in her hair—brought on by stress, most likely—and the darkness under her eyes had deepened a shade or two. "You sleeping much?" He held his umbrella over her head as they walked.

"Yeah. A little here and there. Why?"

"Just checking." Of course he wasn't going to say anything about her appearance. It'd only taken him three ex-wives to learn that lesson.

Sara crossed her arms, tucked her hands into the warmth of her armpits, and leaned further into him under the umbrella. "I look like hell, don't I?"

Barker smirked. "Objection, Your Honor. Leading the witness."

Sara chuckled. It was good to hear that laugh. He wondered how much of that had gone on around the Winthrop household lately. A wild guess said not much on Sara's part.

Settling back into normal didn't mean that memories disappeared. But, post-trauma, she was about as good as she could be, he reckoned. She was surviving, and that coupled with time was all it took a strong person like her to hand the past an ass whooping with an eight-pound sledgehammer.

When they reached the shelter Sara sent the kids off to the other side, told them to use their imaginations and play a game that didn't involve torturing Jacob. She said to Barker, "If that poor boy makes it through high school, I'll be surprised. Do you have sisters?" They sat down on a picnic bench where the wood was faded, gray like the sky, and speckled with pigeon droppings.

Barker shook out his umbrella and pulled it closed. "One older," he said. "Name was Beth and the sweetest woman I ever knew. Well, not when she was younger. Growing up, I'd've been lucky to have your two running the show. They're cupcakes compared to how my sister was way back then. Once we got older, every time I'd go visit and see that bubbly smile, I couldn't help but think that wasn't the girl I grew up with."

"Do you see her much?"

"Nah, she passed about three years ago. Brain tumor took her way too early."

Sara nodded. "It's always too early with something like that."

"Right."

"So what's up, Mr. Bloodhound? Still coming around to make sure I'm sane?" She leaned back, looking past his shoulders. "Jacob, no hanging from the rafters, please!"

"But Mom—"

"I said *no*, and how did you even manage to get up there?"

"Just let me—"

"Down. Now."

Barker watched in amusement as Jacob dropped to a picnic table and hopped down to the concrete flooring. He'd never had children of his own, and seeing other folks deal with theirs made him both regret and applaud his decision. "He's a handful, huh?"

"You want him?" Sara asked. "No charge."

"I'm good, thanks." Barker pulled a cinnamon-flavored toothpick from the breast pocket of his suit coat and tucked it into the corner of his mouth. He'd given up smoking six months ago and so far, so good. Except for that morning. It would've been the perfect sendoff to spark up and blow a plume of smoke in Donald Timms's face.

"Still quit?" Sara asked.

"Yup. I ran two miles yesterday, too."

"Good for you."

"Let me rephrase. I shuffled and coughed up a lung for two miles. Anyway," Barker said, getting up from the picnic table, groaning as he went, feeling the soreness in unused muscles. Tomorrow would be hell. He sighed, put his hands in the pockets of his slacks, and shook his head. He stared out across the playground through the sheets of rain, looking at the tree line across the open soccer field. "Sara, I don't want to do this."

"Do what?" She squinted at him with that questioning look that was a mixture of confusion and get-to-the-point.

"We have…uh…we have a situation, and the suits…well, they wanted me to ask you for help. And I told 'em, I said, no sir, she's been through enough already and I'm not dragging her into something like this. I mean, it's big, like national security big, and there's this guy from the FBI named Donald Timms and he's got perfect hair and the whitest teeth you've ever seen. Real jerk, you know? But he's a Fed and what the Almighty says goes, at least that's the way it works in—"

"Barker…what?" Sara interrupted, slightly shaking her head.

He pinched the bridge of his nose and took a deep breath. "Right. Sorry. I ramble when I get fired up."

"Did I hear you right? Did you say the FBI wants *my* help with something that has to do with national security?"

Barker instinctively reached for a cigarette pack and grumbled when he found the empty spot where they'd been for most of his adult life. Had he quit too soon? Like his nicotine quit coach had said, "There's never a better time than yesterday."

Barker sat down again, planting his rear on the bench this time, below Sara, and looked up at her, shaking his head. "It's the damnedest thing, and I'm still not certain he's telling us the truth. He's shiftier than some of the CIA spooks I've worked with before. Regardless, something's going on, and I have no say in it whatsoever, but they sent me here because we've got history, and they thought you'd be more responsive to the idea if it came from me. Not to mention the fact that you're the expert."

"Expert at what? What idea?"

Barker could sense that she was irritated with him. Hell, he would be too, with all this gibberish, beating around the bush, and not getting to the point. Still, he couldn't come right out and say the words. He knew she'd decline, or try to, so what was the point of asking? And why was he having so much trouble putting the request out there anyway? It wasn't the fear of rejection—he *wanted* her to say no—but maybe it was the thought of bringing up the past and shredding the thin fabric of her stability.

But he could lose his job if he didn't, so the words had to come out, no matter what. Plus, if she said no to him, that wouldn't stop Donald Timms from paying her a visit and utilizing more coercive techniques. The FBI always gets their man, right?

Rather than asking straight up with no background, Barker decided to try a different tactic. "Did you hear about that bombing in London? The one about two months ago?"

"Yeah, it was awful, but what does that have to—"

Barker held up a hand, stopping her. "I'll get there in a second, okay? So, counting back, we got the bombing in London," he said, counting them on his fingers, "the one in Rio, then Beijing before that, and then Moscow. Follow me so far?"

Sara nodded.

"And if I asked you what all four of them had in common, you'd probably say, 'Four bombs exploded and killed a bunch of people,' and you'd be right, but it wouldn't be the right answer. What I'm authorized to tell you—the thing all four of these bombings have in common is—"

Sara gasped. "Cities in *Juggernaut*."

Juggernaut was her employer's top selling game, a first person shooter that had firmly established the company's position as an industry leader.

"True. But it sounds like a stretch to say that they're all connected by a video game. If the Feds only had that to go on, I'd round up every greenhorn, rookie beat cop I could find so they could tell them how stupid the idea was. Hell, I bet we could even ask Jacob and he'd laugh it off."

Sara scooted down from the picnic tabletop and sat on the bench beside Barker. She lowered her voice and had trouble hiding her laughter. "You're saying that the FBI thinks that four terrorist bombings in four random cities are somehow connected by the *Juggernaut* series? I mean, you're kidding, right? Did they hit a dead end already?"

"I know it sounds ridiculous—"

"It's *insane*, Barker."

"—but they think it's a real threat."

"Four *random* cities that just happen to be cities in a video game that I run marketing campaigns for. It's a coincidence. If you're going to count London, Beijing, Moscow, and Rio, then why not Toronto and Cairo? Or Sydney? Or…or Portland, for that matter?"

"That's the thing, Sara. Mr. Timms knows more than he's letting on. I don't know what any of it means, and it could just be a humongous coincidence, but he'd like to talk to you."

"I don't see how I could actually help him, Barker."

"My guess is the asshole wants to use you as bait."

TWO

Quirk blinked and held his breath, concentrating on the two wires in his hands.

A bead of sweat ran down his forehead, arced around his eyebrow, and crawled into the corner of his eye. He cringed at the sting but tried to ignore it. The material on the table in front of him was highly volatile—some new mixture out of the Middle East that his group had managed to procure without too much effort.

After the government had shut down DarkTrade, the world's biggest black market website, and sent the owner to prison, Quirk and his cohorts had to scramble to find a replacement if they were going to stay on schedule.

Luckily, the panic had only lasted about twelve hours before a member of The Clan was able to make a connection. A few illicit transactions through untraceable currency sites, and the package arrived a week later. With all the precautions and safety measures in place by Homeland Security, it still amazed him how easily it was to get something onto U.S. soil if you knew how to do it. Or knew which people could be bribed, bought, or coerced.

With DarkTrade gone, it wasn't like the FBI or the CIA had cut the head off of the snake and that was the end. No, all they did was give rise to twenty more sites just like it, all clamoring to be the new superpower of underworld exchanges.

Drugs, information, weapons, sex…whatever level of debauchery you needed, somebody out there had it for sale. Six months ago, when they'd been prepping for Beijing, Quirk had come across a guy selling, what he claimed to be, one of Hitler's molars. The dude said he had dental records for proof. Quirk doubted the veracity of that claim, but some collector with more money than sense snatched it up for a couple million. For that kind of cash, Quirk had briefly considered yanking out one of his own with a pair of pliers. Surely one of his teeth could pass for Stalin's, couldn't it?

That kind of thinking was old habits dying hard. He didn't need to resort to desperate tactics anymore. Get in with the wrong crowd for the right reason, come with a necessary skill, and watch the decimal places in your bank account launch sideways in a hurry. He'd been careful, subdued, and fully intended to stay invisible as long as possible. No garish purchases like cars or mansions; no flashing stacks of hundreds in strip clubs; no bling…for now—just the simple things that made life a little easier, like paying the bills on time and having something healthier than microwave pizza in the freezer.

If everything went as planned—and he knew it would, because they were meticulous and undetectable—in a year he would be sipping cocktails on a yacht somewhere in the South Pacific. He wouldn't be Mark "Quirk" Ellis anymore. The new Quirk would have a completely clean identity that said he was David Davis, former stock trader that had made millions by betting the right way when the housing bubble had burst.

The Clan had connections, and thus, Quirk had connections.

He twisted the exposed wires together then wrapped a layer of black electrical tape around the mated area. He tucked it inside the casing, gently positioning it around whatever the malleable, explosive material was out of Kabul, Afghanistan, and then secured the bottom of the casing to the laptop. He exhaled a sigh of relief when he righted the device and didn't become hamburger.

Quirk had been assured that the stability was slightly better than the words "highly volatile" suggested and he was in no danger, but you couldn't be too careful when you were working with something exotic. He knew a couple of guys who'd learned that lesson the hard way.

He wiped the sweat from his forehead and trusted his sixth sense.

Good, he thought. *That should do it. Now for the test.*

Quirk turned on the laptop and watched it cycle through the normal boot sequence. He rolled his chair back a couple of inches and turned his head to the side.

As if that would make a difference.

Some self-preservation instincts can't be helped.

The screen cast a blue glow across his face and all seemed normal. It looked like a regular laptop that anyone could be using in a coffee shop while they drank their five-dollar cappuccinos.

This particular work of art could be detonated two different ways. First, by a remote cell signal, his preferred method, and second, a hands-on approach, if his superiors wanted to see a target's face before it evaporated.

They asked him to test it, which he reluctantly agreed to, and if Rocket had programmed the back end correctly, all he had to do was press Enter and then answer with a "Y" or "N" when prompted with the question, "Engage?"

Quirk reached over, held a shaky hand above the

Enter button, made the sign of the cross over his chest, even though he wasn't Catholic, and lowered his finger—

An annoying ringtone blared on the table beside the lamp. Quirk cursed and backed away from the bomb, then picked up the disposable phone and spat out a greeting. "What?"

"Is this Quirk?"

He didn't recognize the voice. Only three people had the number and whoever this was, she wasn't one of them. Protocol and common sense said to hang up, but he had a feeling that that wouldn't be wise. "Who's asking?"

"Boudica."

Every muscle in Quirk's body clenched. Part nervous reaction, part fear…all valid. Boudica, leader of The Clan, named after a Celtic queen who had led a bloody uprising against the Romans a couple thousand years ago, was ruthless, emotionless, and so, so dangerous. He'd never met her in person, but Quirk was absolutely certain that he had no desire to meet Boudica in a McDonald's or a dark alley, ever.

He stammered, "Oh—*oh*, right. How did you get—I mean, who—so, uh, what's up?" Quirk shook his head and rolled his eyes.

'What's up?' Really?

"What's up," Boudica said, "is my blood pressure, Captain Quirk."

Quirk stifled a chuckle. Captain Quirk. He'd heard rumors that she had a sense of humor when she was in a good mood—which was rare, apparently—and temporarily considered making some sort of comment about the *Enterprise*, but decided against it. "We don't want that," he replied.

"No, we don't. Rocket tells me you're close. Are you still on schedule?"

"I don't mean to brag, but I'm ahead, actually. Putting on the finishing touches just now and was about to test the initiation sequence."

"Perfect, because we're moving it up a week."

Quirk nearly dropped the cell phone. He stood up and knocked his head on the low-hanging light. It danced around and sent erratic shadows flailing throughout the room. "A week? I'm not so sure that's a—I mean, we should do more testing and I don't know how well this stuff travels, and there are a lot of things that could—"

"Next Tuesday, Quirk. No questions."

He'd become a hermit over the past forty-eight hours and had stayed so secluded and detached from reality that he had trouble remembering what day it was, if it was light outside, or if the digital time display above his desk was AM or PM. He double-checked and realized it was seven o'clock Saturday morning, which meant—"That's way too soon. Will all the pieces be in place by then?"

"Are you questioning my judgment?"

"No, honest to God, I'm not, Boudica...Miss Boudica...ma'am. Um, it's just that, well, I'm sure you remember what happened in London."

"I do. And whose fault was that?"

"Mine, sort of, but not completely, because—"

"It won't happen again, will it, Quirk?"

"No, ma'am." Quirk felt that morning's breakfast of Mountain Dew and candy corn roiling in his stomach. Bright idea at the time; he'd needed the dual-action caffeine blast and sugar rush to keep from face-planting into Kabul's finest unstable putty. But now the concoction of soda and sugar felt like syrupy acid bubbling up and melting his insides.

"I didn't think so. Now, here's what I want you to do. Crawl out of that little cave you call a workshop, shower, dress, whatever, and make yourself presentable, then I want you to meet with Cleo down at Powell's, okay?"

Quirk agreed, but wondered why she wanted them to meet in such a public place.

Boudica answered the unasked question for him.

"You two Portland hipsters will blend in to the crowd there, so it'll be a perfect place to scout undetected. Flannel, skinny jeans, just look like you belong, got me? She'll brief you on the new details."

The skin on his arms prickled. "Are we doing the drop *there*?"

Before, their targets had been low-key places. Sure, they'd resulted in some casualties, but they were considered collateral damage and merely an aspect of the objective they were trying to accomplish. Regardless of what the latest scientific study reported, violent video games like the *Juggernaut* series led to an increase in violent behavior in children, and the population of Earth needed to see that on a much grander scale.

The way things worked in the world, some kid would get shot in rural Oklahoma and people would blame it on the hottest new first person shooter, which might cause it to be newsworthy for about twenty-four hours, only to be replaced by the next major headline: "Celebutante names baby girl after fruit."

However, if somebody raised the stakes to the point where it could no longer be ignored, then surely some regulatory commissions would be formed. Someone would pay attention.

Every member of The Clan, from Boudica on

down to the delivery driver, Tank, was a former gamer who'd lost a close friend or family member to video game violence. The propagandists insisted the phenomenon didn't exist. They insisted that blood, guts, guns, bullets, and scattered body parts flashing across the screen and into young minds were no more harmful than watching Jerry the mouse smash Tom the cat over the head with a mallet.

Boudica cleared her throat. She was angry now, and there would be no more jokes about Captain Quirk. "I'm starting to think your commitment might not be at the level we need."

"No, no, I'm cool—"

"Cool? I don't care if you're a penguin on an iceberg. Are you in this one hundred percent or not, Quirk?"

"Yes, ma'am. All the way."

"And I don't need to send him in?"

"Him? No. God, no. Please. I wasn't questioning you or anything like that—you caught me off guard. I wasn't expecting things to escalate so quickly." And especially not right here in his backyard. Not right in the heart of downtown Portland.

The "him" she was referring to was Boudica's own version of a black-ops cleaner. In the two years The Clan had been planning and executing missions, the

Spirit had been necessary only once, when a financier of theirs had threatened exposure. In their smoky back-room meetings and secret chat rooms, no one had been able to figure out why. They made no profit off their illicit behaviors. Didn't want financial gain, didn't need financial gain. Their objective was information. So why had this guy Alvarez tried to blackmail them? He had nothing to achieve.

The only suggestion that made even the slightest bit of sense was a lover's quarrel, and if Boudica had no issues with having someone eliminated that she'd shared bodily fluids with, then scraping an uncooperative Quirk off the bottom of her shoe would be a small checkmark on her list.

All Quirk and the other members need to stay loyal and subservient was one look at the gruesome pictures of Alvarez following the Spirit's work, accompanied by a message to think before they acted.

Boudica said, "*Your* job, Quirk, is to make things go *boom. My* job is to make sure people pay attention. You worry about your job, I'll worry about mine."

Quirk mumbled in agreement, but that was it. He was positive that no matter what words came out of his mouth, they'd be misconstrued and he'd wake up in the middle of the night with that familiar stranger hovering over him.

Boudica added, "Powell's at ten. You'll remember Cleo when you see her, won't you?"

"Yes," Quirk said, thinking, *How could I forget?*

THREE

There weren't enough chairs in the small office to accommodate the silent, waiting crowd. For most of them, it wasn't the way they'd intended to spend their Saturday. They had better things to do than stand in an unrented office on the third floor of a downtown Portland high-rise.

The previous occupants had left behind a desk, four chairs, and a whiteboard.

Sara had asked why they didn't meet somewhere that made sense. Barker had only been able to shrug and say that it was what Timms had requested.

Sitting on the opposite side of the desk in his usual position of authority, the President, CEO, and chief motivator of LightPulse Technologies reclined in the high-backed leather chair and tented his fingertips. He brought the forefingers up to his lips and then rested his chin on the thumbs below. He appeared to be lost in thought, but Sara knew it wasn't true. Jim Rutherford was never *lost* when he was doing anything.

Whatever turned the gears inside that skull housed under a thin sheet of salt and pepper hair had to be some brilliant plan full of such devious machinations that this so-called terrorist group would be wise to tuck tail and vanish. Sara hoped so, at least. From the way the conversation had gone so far, she'd gotten the vibe that LightPulse was more of a target than she was bait, as Barker had assumed.

Jim was dressed in his standard outfit of jeans, sneakers, and a black turtleneck, which now was more of a tribute to Steve Jobs than some subtle attempt to emulate the late tech giant.

To Jim's left, leaning against the window with his arms crossed and one leg halfway propped up on a short table, was Teddy Rutherford, Sara's former (and sometimes current) nemesis.

He was Jim's privileged son, and had also managed to survive the wrath of Shelley Sergeant and her massive, intimidating, and morose brother, Michael. But not without a few broken bones and blackened bruises that took weeks to disappear. Sara had saved Teddy's life and occasionally wondered why, especially when he was having too much fun being…well, *Teddy*.

Thank God for small miracles, because he was in a cooperative mood, which could've been due to the presence of Karen Wallace, the private investigator that Jim kept on retainer after Sara's incident. She sat to Barker's left, and Teddy didn't have to turn his head more than a couple of degrees to ogle her.

And why shouldn't he? She was tall, beautiful, highly intelligent, well spoken, had a concealed-carry permit, and didn't want a damn thing to do with his too-polished, bronzer-coated melon. Her lack of interest fueled Teddy's need to chase, however futile the possibilities.

Agent Donald Timms of the FBI, whom Sara knew nothing about, stood to the left of Karen, next to the inter-office windows that looked into an empty hallway, where doors led to other empty offices.

Timms seemed distracted and bored by having to mingle with the mortals while he briefed them of details. Underneath his professional exterior was a layer of creepiness that didn't sit right with Sara.

In reality he was probably fine, but call it a mother's intuition, whatever the case, she wasn't sure she'd leave her children alone in a room with the guy.

Six people total, five of them waiting on Jim Rutherford to say something.

Anything.

Jim leaned forward and opened his mouth, then sank back into his seat.

Timms finally spoke. "I'm sure you understand there are time considerations."

Jim flicked a dismissive glance at him, followed it with an eye roll, and said to Teddy, "Did you see this coming?"

Teddy gulped, stammered, and shrugged, reacting as if he'd been caught dipping into Daddy's liquor cabinet. "Me, no… I—this is… Sara's the one who—"

Sara uncrossed her legs, leaned forward with her elbows on her knees, and stared at Teddy. Eyebrows raised, lips pinched tightly together, head angled to one side as if to say, *Sara's the one who* what, *you little shit?*

Teddy nodded an acknowledgment. He knew better. The days of passing the blame were gone. Same team. Don't mess with the badass chick.

He continued, "There's no way that we could've predicted this. Sara and I are involved in development and marketing. How could *we* have seen it coming? And for that matter, why would any of these bombs be specifically related to LightPulse? That's all I'm asking."

"And you're asking it so clearly." Barker smirked and waggled the toothpick in his mouth.

Teddy pushed himself away from the window and reasserted his position with his hands on his hips. "You know what I mean."

"Maybe."

Timms cleared his throat. "If I may?"

Jim ignored him and said to Sara, "What're your thoughts?"

"If I may, sir?" Timms repeated.

"You may not," Jim said. Unruffled, without making eye contact, and staring at a hangnail instead, he added, "Agent Timms, I don't care if you're J. Edgar himself. You bring us here under clandestine pretenses, insinuating that my company, my games, and my employees are responsible for these atrocities…I'm not a fan of it. So I'd like to ask my associates some questions before I decide whether or not to give merit to your ludicrous claims."

"We have evidence this is related to LightPulse. The informants all say…"

Jim held up a hand and Timms let his words trail off into frustrated silence.

Sara wondered how long he'd put up with Jim's posturing before he began asserting some federal dominance. *Whose is bigger, boys? Who cares? Put them away; there are more important issues to discuss.*

"Sara?"

She looked at Barker and managed to nod and shake her head at the same time. "Detective Barker could only tell me so much, but honestly, Jim, I don't have the slightest clue. I'm sure Agent Timms can speak more to this—"

"I can, if you'll let me—"

"—but the only connection we can see at this level is the fact that they're all cities in *Juggernaut*. It could easily be the same for ProVision's *Task Force Delta* or…what's the other one, Teddy?"

"*Black Wing Fighter*. GameCon."

"Right, *BWF*."

Jim said, "Not necessarily. GameCon moved away from the global playing area with *BWF*. They didn't have the workforce to keep that exhaustive level of development up."

"Still," Sara reminded him, "London, Beijing…all the cities that have been hit were there in their previous versions."

Jim and Teddy nodded in agreement.

Karen Wallace was finally kind enough to interject and give Timms the chance to speak. As a former FBI agent herself, having left the spit-polished life of federal investigation for the more lucrative world of public enterprise, she was sympathetic to him, yet slightly pleased by the fact that he probably wasn't used to being so dismissed.

She said, "Before we get too far into the whys, I'd like to hear what Timms knows. Is that okay with you, Jim?"

Jim nodded curtly; a short, do-as-you-must resignation.

Timms dipped his chin in thanks and stepped over to the whiteboard.

He picked up a blue marker, wrote the names of the cities where the attacks had occurred, and said, "The responsible group is now saying that these attacks are to prove a point, that video games lead to violent behavior, ergo, detonations and casualties around the world. It's a bit ironic, isn't it? Blowing things up to draw attention to youth violence? Anyway, London, Rio, Beijing, Moscow…you've all been briefed on what seems like a flimsy, superficial connection to your *Juggernaut* series by the good Detective Barker here. As far as we know, that's all it is. Coincidence.

"These are major cities in the world where a lot happens, so it stands to reason that yes, it's an insubstantial correlation. If I'm familiar enough with the concept of your game; the bombings could've been in any major metropolis and it still would've made a sliver of a connection to *Juggernaut.* However, that's not what brings me here. Something definitely happened in these cities…something that ties itself to LightPulse in a roundabout way." He finished by underlining each city name and tapping the board beside them. "And, contrary to what you might believe, the FBI isn't omnipotent—"

Barker chuckled and interrupted, "Could've fooled me."

Timms said, "Despite Barker's misgivings about our capabilities, *at first*, this string of bombings looked like nothing more than the work of a random terrorist group. We figured it was the usual suspects like Al Qaeda or any number of Middle Eastern extremist groups that aren't big enough or well-funded enough to catch the public's attention. But there were dead ends all around. None of them stepped forward to take credit for the attacks, nor did we have any false claims like we typically do."

Teddy asked, "You get a lot of those?"

"More than we'd like, since the required manpower to follow up on those leads can be limited, but they usually check out fake and we overlook them like some new kid trying to make a name for himself on the playground. It was unusual, honestly, because we typically get at least one camp that sends a message from their cave in Afghanistan, but not this time."

Karen raised a hand and didn't wait for Timms to acknowledge her. "Why do you think that is?"

Timms shrugged. "We don't know. It doesn't make any sense to us, either. The only thing that our exploratory teams can assume—"

Barker said, "Ass out of you and me."

"The only thing that makes sense is that the attacks were initially too small and they figured it wasn't worth their time. If you're a tiny group trying to get attention, it doesn't make a big enough impression if all you did was blow up a GameStop and recorded no casualties. On the opposite side of that, if you're Al Qaeda, it's beneath you. See where I'm going with this? Al Qaeda is in the business of trying to upset the world balance, not trying to disintegrate a couple of Playstations. We rounded up every informant we could find that was familiar with this style of work and none of them had anything new for us. We figured we'd start with the tangibles—the concrete evidence we had to go on. The bomb maker, whoever he may be, is military trained, but his signatures aren't consistent enough for us to determine by *whose* military. We think he's a former U.S. Marine, but he could just as easily be Israeli Intelligence."

Barker said, "I thought we were friends with the Israelis?"

"And a former Marine used to bleed red, white, and blue. What's your point?"

"What's yours?"

"He's clever enough to hide his tracks well, but the

traces he's left behind suggest friendly fire, Detective."

Sara stood and joined Timms at the whiteboard. "So basically what you're telling us is that you have no idea who these people are, but for some unknown reason you think their motives are tied to *our* games."

"That's…not entirely true."

"Then what *is* true, Agent Timms? Did you just pick LightPulse out of a hat, or are you going from office to office, hoping something might stick out enough for you to latch onto it? Because, believe me, you asked for *my* help specifically, but I am *not* interested in getting involved in something like this if it's nothing more than a random assumption. Not after the year I've had. I don't know if Detective Barker filled you in on my situation or not—"

"He did."

"—but I'm definitely not prepared to help you go looking for something that may not exist, especially if it's going to put my children in danger again—or Teddy, for that matter."

Teddy grinned. "Thanks, Sara."

"Mrs. Winthrop," Timms said, "you won't be in any kind of danger. That's a promise."

"Promises are broken. Can you guarantee it?"

"Fine, I guarantee that you won't be in any danger."

"Uh-huh, right," she said, not believing a word of it. "Detective Barker here thought you were up to something, so why me? Why not Jim or Teddy? I mean, I'm sorry, guys," Sara said, looking at the father and son, "I'm not trying to throw you under the bus, but you know just as much as I do about *Juggernaut*, if not more. Right?"

Timms picked up the whiteboard eraser and scrubbed away his scribbling. "Because of this." He wrote seven names on the board: "Boudica," "Chief," "Rocket," "Quirk," "Sharkfin," "Tank," and "Cleo."

"Yeah," Sara said, "they're the names of characters in *Juggernaut*. So what? Did you read the instruction manual before you came in?"

"We've identified these seven people as members of a small organization called The Clan. From what we know, they're former gamers, hackers, and scumbags."

"And that relates to me how?"

"It took us a few weeks of digging around in the deepest corners of the internet to come up with something concrete. Using our informants, we started putting out feelers for anything related to these bombings in particular. People talk. People are always talking. They like being in the know, they like having information to share because it gives them a sense of authority. I'd say the two biggest things that have changed world history are sex and that childish sense of hoarding information."

"They like the money, too," Barker added.

"I can't confirm that money is exchanged for information, but…you know."

Teddy stepped around the office desk and sauntered to the back of the room, grinning.

Timms said, "Something funny, Mr. Rutherford?"

"I'm not saying I know this for certain," Teddy said, shrugging. "I mean…the FBI may have the brightest and sharpest people working for them that money can buy, yet they don't hold a candle to some of the hackers and gamers out there that never finished high school. I'm sure you know that and have probably tried to recruit them. I would be willing to bet my stock in LightPulse that there's some MIT graduate living in his mom's basement, chugging Red Bull and surviving on Ramen who hasn't seen the sun for days—he's out there running circles around your Ivy League robots."

"Meaning?"

Teddy glanced at Karen Wallace, smirking. Posturing. Showing off his plumage, hoping that, eventually, the mating call would work. He said, "You can't be that naïve, can you? Seriously, if you found these people through some underground network on the internet, it's only because they *wanted* you to find them. And…*and*, they probably know which analyst did it and what shoe size he wears."

Sara shrugged. "Teddy's probably right."

"Oh, we're aware," Timms said, sneering. "Which is part of the reason I'm here to talk to *you*, Mrs. Winthrop."

FOUR

Quirk didn't wait for the crosswalk sign to change. He ignored the bright orange hand and dashed across the street, hearing the polite *beep* of a hybrid Honda's horn, rather than a wailing honk. That was one of the many things he loved about Portland. The sheer niceness that emanated from every pore of environmentally conscious skin and oozed from every crack in the sidewalk.

Portland was so much different than his native New York City. The dreaded visits home had become fewer with more time between them as the years had passed. He hadn't been back to Long Island since his brother Alan came home from Iraq with a flag draped over the casket.

That was four years ago. Two years ago, after Alan's widow, Melissa, had packed up and moved, heartbroken, back to North Carolina, his nephew had died from a gunshot wound to the chest. Brandon had been buried on a rainy afternoon. Quirk would never forget that day.

The courts, in their infinite wisdom, had ruled it an accident, but Quirk knew better. All the signs of bullying and violence, brought on by video games, were there. All the signs were overlooked.

Brandon was twelve years old when his father died. He buried himself in online gaming to hide from the pain, because what else do teen boys do? "Feelings" are reserved for bad poetry, written to the cute girl in class who won't offer a second glance—feelings weren't meant for anyone that might actually listen and help.

Though he lived three thousand miles away, Quirk had tried to make a connection with his nephew. They spent hours online together, chatting over headsets, playing *Juggernaut*, and Quirk thought he'd reached a breakthrough.

Brandon had become more willing to open up about missing his father, but not long after, he'd complained about some kids from school that were bullying him during rounds of online gaming when Quirk wasn't there to listen in.

Six months later, during what was supposed to be a fun, live-action reenactment of *Juggernaut* organized by the same kids that were pushing him around, Brandon took a bullet to the chest and died on the way to the hospital. The shooter's excuse—"I didn't know it was loaded"—sent Brandon's murderer walking out of the courtroom a free man. Or, a free boy, rather.

Quirk was positive that he was the only one to notice the subtle grin on the little prick's face.

Quirk tracked Bobby Marlowe down one night, managed to work himself into the conversation among the young gaming teammates, and overheard the kid bragging about what he'd done. "You should've seen him," Marlowe had said. "His chest exploded like those little purple alien bastards."

No one believed Quirk. No one would listen. He never let it go. Instead it sat heavy in his stomach, the revenge gestating, waiting for the right opportunity.

Quirk knew the boy was too young, a fourteen-year-old child, but he could wait. Four more years and adulthood would come soon enough. In the meantime, dedicating his talents to The Clan's objective would help pass the time, and, hopefully, draw much-needed attention to the cause.

He stopped beneath the overhang outside of Powell's, pinched the loose material of his nylon windbreaker, and shook it, relieving it from the drops of rain. He took off his skullcap, tucked it into an open pocket, and then tried to mash down his wayward hair.

Quirk caught his reflection in the window. Full beard, brown with flecks of red and traces of blond. A couple of gray ones, too. Those had grown rampant in recent months.

He examined the rounded eyeglasses and unkempt hair. Skinny jeans that hugged the wrong parts in the wrong places and a pair of Chuck Taylors. Flannel shirt underneath the blue windbreaker.

Yeah, he thought, *I look hipster enough. Blending in, like Boudica said.*

It wasn't his style, really, especially not at thirty-eight years old and as a former bomb disposal tech for the United States Marine Corps, but hiding in plain sight with the northwestern camouflage was the easiest route. And besides, Cleo defined hipster. She would appreciate his Portland chic.

Quirk waited for a couple of minutes, anxiously pacing, debating whether to go inside or stand his ground. He checked the time on his cell. She was either late or already among the stacks of books, waiting for him. Just as he was about to turn and push through the door, he felt a hand on his arm. At the same time, he heard the voice of his daydreams. Not so much the voice, exactly, but the woman it belonged to. "Quirk?"

He turned to face her. It'd been a while, but infatuation has a way of warping time, and he remembered her features as if they'd had coffee together that morning.

She was different, but the same.

Her hair was blonde now with blue highlights,

shorter—a pixie cut—and a better length and color than the pink bob that she'd had the last time they were together. The hoop in her left nostril had been replaced with a small diamond stud that matched the new addition of a diamond stud in her bottom lip. He didn't need to survey everything about her. He could've drawn a perfect portrait of her from memory, but he liked admiring what he hoped would be his one day. Maybe she liked yachts and the South Pacific.

Quirk shook his head. Had he been staring too long? "Cleo, hi. Good to see you again." He offered his hand to shake and when she took it he felt a warm glow race up his arm and down through his legs.

Those full lips. Wide brown eyes that penetrated everything they focused on. She didn't just see things; she absorbed them. The beautiful row of upper teeth flashed when she smiled and he was glad to see that the left incisor was still a little crooked. Cleo's tiny imperfections were all minor subplots of her new age narrative.

She wore black-rimmed glasses, rectangular in shape, and the color contrasted nicely against her Portland tan, which was to say, alabaster white.

The rest of her attire surprised him. The white top was button-down and collared, followed by a gray pencil skirt and what he supposed were sensible heels.

Cleo looked...professional. Mainstream.

Cleo wasn't her real name, of course. It was a call sign, just like "Quirk" and "Boudica." In real life she was Emily Armstrong, but he wasn't supposed to know that. It could be dangerous if she found out and told Boudica, but the thousand dollars he'd offered some kid on DarkTrade to dig up information had been worth every penny.

Quirk shook her hand long enough to feel the slight tug, the pulling away, that uncomfortable moment of, 'Okay, enough already.'

He said, "You look...great."

Cleo shrugged. "New job," she said. "I'm lucky I get away with the dye and the piercings."

Quirk was already aware of her new position as a bank teller for Wells Fargo. Good for her. Working as a bartender for that strip joint, Mary's, had probably paid better in tips, but the hours were horrible and bad for her health.

He thought about asking why she even bothered to work. If the money from Boudica showed up in the offshore bank account each time for her like it did for him after every successful mission, then she should already be well on her way to freedom from Corporate America and The Man. As far as he could tell, and from what he'd learned while observing her, she simply enjoyed keeping herself busy.

"Well," he said, "they're lucky to have you," earning him an odd look.

Too much, Quirk, dial it down.

To Cleo, they were practically strangers, having met once eighteen months ago in Moscow to scout their first location. Their encounter was brief, but the impression was lasting. They'd posed as a young couple on their honeymoon; they were in, they were out, a used videogame store exploded three days later, and Quirk was in love.

He coughed into his fist and held the door open for her.

She thanked him and walked inside, saying, "Sorry I'm late. I had a friend drop me off, and she wouldn't be on time for her own funeral."

Quirk chuckled and followed her into the miraculous hub of Powell's, Reading Central, one of his favorite places in the city, and in life.

Every city deserved a place brimming with as much awesomeness and goodwill as Powell's. Stories, words, and worlds were introduced to the masses like screaming babies fresh from the womb, or they were given new life, resurrected with that defibrillator known as the enjoyment of a well told tale.

The bottom floor of Powell's was the Orange

Level, reminding Quirk of the now-retired terror alert chart put in place by Homeland Security after 9/11. Back then, Orange meant the risk of terrorist activity was high, and given the reason why he and Cleo were there, it fit perfectly.

Cleo reached down and took his hand, locking her fingers with his. "Just like old times," she said. All business, with not a hint of actual nostalgia. "Over here." She pulled; Quirk followed.

Saturday mornings at Powell's were a perfect time to get lost in the crowd. The place hummed with electric excitement. Shoppers carried bags of books. Some pushed carts. They sipped coffee. They browsed for hours while children raced up and down the aisles searching for their parents, begging for this book or that story.

It was one of Quirk's favorite ways to lose an entire day, and it saddened him that after the following Tuesday he might not get another chance.

Cleo tugged his hand and he trailed after her, down a row of business books that was surprisingly empty of browsers. She whispered, "Why?"

"You mean why here?"

Cleo stepped closer. Her perfume smelled like cotton candy. Quirk swooned on the inside. She said, "Why's she changing the plan, huh? Moving it up a week, picking a new place? Doesn't that seem strange to you?"

Quirk nodded. "Totally."

She glanced past his shoulder and mouthed, "Wait," and turned his body with a subtle nudge. The young woman ten feet to their right looked, found what she wanted, and left them alone again. "Okay, she's gone. So what's the deal, do you know?"

"I didn't find out until this morning."

"I mean, I'm in, all the way, but it kinda freaks me out. Doesn't it freak you out? What if somebody's onto us and she's trying to push the agenda before we're ready?"

"You think so?"

"If somebody's onto us, they could have us under surveillance right now. It could've been that chick. Or it could be that guy over there in the purple sweater."

Quirk squeezed her hand. "Don't freak, okay? We're fine. If somebody made us, like the cops or the FBI, we'd already be in cuffs."

"Or they could be giving us just enough rope to hang ourselves with."

"True. I guess the question is who're you more afraid of? The cops or Boudica?"

Cleo pulled her hand free from his, bit her bottom lip, and scratched her head. Crossing her arms under the perfect breasts that Quirk fantasized about on a nightly basis, she said, "We both know the answer to that."

"Right." He glanced away before she could notice him staring at her chest.

"Which means we should probably do our jobs."

Quirk pushed his glasses higher on his nose. "I'll go up top. Start down here and we'll make our way through, then meet back in this aisle in an hour. You remember what to look for, don't you?"

"Yeah, we're looking for places with low traffic but near something structural."

"Good, you remember. Honestly, I don't think it's going to matter much, not with this new stuff we've got. We leave the package on a shelf right here on the ground floor—it'll bring the whole place down. Better safe than sorry, and we should still check it out, so maybe you should watch the patterns of the employees more than trying to find a good drop point. Make sense?"

"I guess, but this is a little different than a few small shops on the other side of the world, Quirk. For God's sake, this is Powell's. It's an institution, and we could potentially…you know, there could be hundreds of them."

Them. Casualties.

"Do you think we could convince her to go for some other place?"

"Would you even have the balls to try?"

He shook his head.

"Then we don't have a choice."

FIVE

Sara stepped away from the whiteboard and returned to her seat beside Barker.

Timms made her anxious on a number of different levels, and retreating to Barker's proximity felt like the comforting thing to do. At twenty years older, roughly, maybe it was some sort of protective father-figure association. Regardless, his masculine mustache and swagger seemed to keep Timms lurking on the perimeter.

She said, "So is this a need-to-know thing, or are you actually going to tell us how I'm connected or why I need to be a part of it?"

Timms placed the cap back on the marker and dropped it into the tray. "I hadn't planned on doing it in a room full of people, to be perfectly honest. But Barker's superiors—and yours, and, unfortunately, mine—have assured me that this level of cooperation is necessary and the only way of getting what we want."

"Cut the bullshit," Barker said. "If this is a matter of national security and not a single one of us in here has any level of clearance, then how in the hell do you expect us to cooperate or help?"

Karen added, "My clearance expired. Jim, Teddy, and Sara have never had any government clearance that I know of, and given what I remember, protocol dictates that we should—"

Timms raised his voice, speaking over Karen, "I don't care what protocol dictates, Miss Wallace, we're in a unique situation here and some of the rules are meant to be bent and broken. Happens all the time."

"I'm just saying—"

"You're out of the game. Leave the FBI's business to those that are actually still employed by them, okay? Sound fair to you?"

Karen crossed her arms and looked away. Teddy moved up behind her and Sara noticed him internally debating on whether or not to put a comforting hand on the private investigator's shoulder. Wisely, he decided against it.

Jim said to Timms, "My turn to remind *you*, Agent—there are time considerations here. Get on with it, please. No need to keep beating our chests."

"I completely agree with you, sir. Now, if you'll allow me to finish before asking questions, that would be helpful. Agreed? Everyone? Detective Barker, can we agree on that small courtesy? Good."

Barker winked at Sara. She hid her smile behind a manufactured cough.

Timms continued, "Like the younger Mr. Rutherford so helpfully suggested, we knew going into this that our analysts wouldn't likely escape undetected with the information we needed. There are kids out there, fifteen, sixteen years old, that are brilliant enough to match wits with our top-notch players. It's unfortunate, but we can do nothing about it—well, except for arresting and recruiting them. So rather than trying to sneak in like a bunch of cyber-ninjas and have the whole internet community point and laugh at us like the poor chubby kid at school, we use our informants.

"Miss Wallace and Detective Barker are familiar with this method, I'm sure. You've all seen it on television. That's not to say that we don't have some associates in deep cover, but they're the exception to the rule. Anyway. Our informants found traces of chatter that originated with the most recent event in London and they managed to trace the chain of communication all the way back to the first event in Moscow."

Sara felt some disdain at the word "event," and the nonchalant usage, as if it were a party or an annual convention instead of an explosion that claimed lives.

Timms continued, "Now, again, as Teddy suggested, it appears as if they *wanted* to be found. These most recent tracks had to have been laid on purpose like Hansel and Gretel on their way to the oven. It was too sloppy. They'd been so careful and, I don't know, *hygienic* in their methods before—a group with their caliber of talent doesn't suddenly become a bunch of bumbling idiots."

"Why would they do that?" Karen asked.

"That's the billion-dollar question, isn't it? Misdirection is the most likely reason. The crumb trail shows no indication that they were in any sort of fear whatsoever that we were onto them. They communicated primarily through untraceable, disposable cell phones in short bursts to avoid any attempts at triangulation, and they used private chat rooms with such an intense system of rerouting that it froze one of our servers trying to trace them. Then, one day, *poof*, it's like they held up a flashing neon sign saying, 'Hey, we're over here!' So that tells us one of two things: either they have a mole inside and they knew we were getting close, or they rolled one of the informants."

Teddy said, "How?"

"Crime pays better than our measly stipends. This is all speculation, of course, but The Clan, which is made up of these seven individuals, they decided that they'd throw themselves out there and offer up information about their next attack, hoping to misdirect us while they went after their actual target."

"Hold on now," Barker said, scooting forward in his chair. "If these dipshits are as smart as you *say* they are, wouldn't it occur to them that it would set off a bunch of alarm bells if all of a sudden they made a huge, honking screw-up after they'd been faultless for so long?"

"Exactly, Detective. Maybe you'd make it in the FBI after all."

"Don't bet on it. Square isn't my favorite shape." Karen and Teddy laughed.

Timms ignored the barb. "We think it's a double-double misdirection."

"Is that your official term?"

"No, I came up with that all by myself, Detective, and I thought we agreed to hold questions until I was finished?"

"*We*," Barker said, pointing at the side of his head, "agreed to no such thing, but in the interest of having lunch before sundown, I'll concede."

"How generous of you."

"Don't mention it."

Getting back to the case, Timms said, "The

general consensus is that one, they knew we'd pick up on the fact that this misstep was intentional. Two, the intent was to make us think there were ulterior motives behind it and convince us to look elsewhere. By blatantly telling us what their next target would be, they hoped we'd ignore the fact that they were going to blow up exactly what they told us would be the next target."

Jim said, "I'm sorry, Agent, I don't follow."

Before Timms could answer him, Teddy said, "It's like that cutaway scene in *Troll Towers* where Balthazar says he's going to punch Grogg the Cruel with his left hand, so Grogg dodges left, thinking he's coming from the right, and then Balthazar levels him with that left hook and goes, 'I told you.' Right? Remember that, Sara?"

Sara nodded. "I do, Teddy," she said, slightly bemused at the manchild's nostalgic excitement for a game that was over a decade old—one he'd helped write the storyline for back before he even officially began working for LightPulse.

"My sons played that game," Timms said, "but yes, I think that's about as close of a comparison as I can come up with. Does that work for you, Mr. Rutherford?"

Jim sighed. "I suppose. Continue."

"No, hang on," Barker said. "So you're saying that this group came right out and *told* you what their next target was going to be, hoping you'd look for something else?"

"It looks that way, yes."

"Again, I gotta ask...don't you think they'd be smart enough to know you'd figure *that* out, too?"

"Possibly, but we can go around and around with the whole, 'I know you know that I know that you know,' thing. Eventually you have to pick a direction and go."

"What did they say the target was?" Sara asked.

"The CBOE. The Chicago Board of Exchange."

"Then why're you here? Why aren't you in Chicago trying to stop them there?"

"Because it's not the actual target."

"But you said they came right out and told you what it was."

"I did."

Frustrated, Sara barely managed to contain her anger. "Then what's the goddamn target, Timms? Why are you here? Why am *I* here?"

Teddy's voice was low and somber, so different than his usual hyper tone and energy. He said, "Oh God, it's somewhere in Portland, isn't it?"

Timms nodded. He took off his suit jacket and

draped it across the coat rack. He rolled up his sleeves. "The problem is, we need to figure out where."

Barker said, "We're not doing anything until you explain how you figured out that the next target was here instead of Chicago when they deliberately *said* it was there."

"That, Detective, is where the need-to-know comes in. My superiors asked for discretion and I'm ordered to comply. Of course, I could tell you—"

"—but then you'd have to kill me. Right. Fish and squirrels may fly, but that doesn't make them birds, Timms."

"Huh?"

"Never mind. Either you show the cards you're holding, or I take Mrs. Winthrop out of here. She hasn't officially agreed to anything yet, and besides, don't think I haven't noticed. You keep beating around the bush, promising to give us information, but you really haven't told us a damn thing about why you need to have her involved. So if it's all the same to you— and Sara, if you'll allow me to speak for you here—pull that curtain to the side, Oz, or we walk, end of story."

Timms mulled it over. Sara wondered if he was debating on how much trouble he'd be in if he disobeyed direct orders. Barker had him by the balls. Timms knew it, and so did everyone else in the room.

Five against one. They waited.

He pulled a handkerchief from his pocket and dabbing at his forehead, he said, "Fine. In the interest of saving lives…this does not leave this office. Are we understood? Especially you, Barker. If I happen to catch even the slightest hint that you're out there on Twitter blabbing secrets of the Federal Bureau of Investigation, you'll be spending what limited time you have left trying to survive in a cell with some guy who you probably put there in the first place. Are we clear?"

"Crystal. But one question…"

"What?"

"What's a Twitter?"

Everyone but Timms and Barker laughed. Barker may have been poking fun at himself, but if he was, he held the befuddled expression like a pro.

Timms put his hands on Jim's desk and leaned forward. Looking at Sara, he asked, "Do you remember a woman named Patricia Kellog?"

The name brought back a flood of memories. Junior year of high school, wanting so badly to be popular, to make a good impression on the cheerleaders at Washington High so she could join the upper echelon of coolness. Being part of the crowd that ruled the school was important back then. It meant all the awesome parties, the cutest boys, sharing the best clothes, and being worshipped by the scrubs walking the halls.

She'd changed, obviously. Growing up, growing older and wiser, realizing how idiotic but unavoidable the whole process was for a bunch of teens thrown together, coming into themselves, trying to figure out their place in life.

Patricia Kellog. Patty. Batty Patty. Patty the Fatty.

Old regrets hit the hardest.

Sara had plenty of them—she wasn't perfect. Who was? Yet the one that she'd subconsciously worked so hard to bury in her mind was that night at the homecoming game. Sara hadn't done the actual deed, but she was guilty of laughing to look cool while on the inside she had pleaded for them to stop. The incident was enough to change her opinions about what it took to wear the crown of supreme popularity, and she moved on. There were better ways to live her life.

Sara said, "She left high school during our junior year. I haven't seen her since. The last I heard, she spent some time in a mental hospital."

And I never got the chance to apologize, she thought. *We were dumb, cruel kids.*

"Right," Timms said, "and her former psychiatrists informed me that her stay wasn't a pleasant one." He pointed at the whiteboard. “See that name up there on the top of the list?”

“Boudica?”

“Meet Patty Kellog.”

SIX

With their recon complete, Quirk and Cleo found each other in the business section again. Rather, Quirk spotted Cleo first and took his time on the approach. Her pencil skirt stopped just below the knee and when she turned away, unaware of him, pretending to browse books on a different shelf, he noticed that it zipped in the back, all the way up to her waist. The short gap between the zipper and the hem provided a tiny glimpse into the unknown that resided above, and he had to shake his mind free of the lustful images that followed.

Job first, Quirk. White picket fence later. This is for Brandon, not your libido.

He stopped at the entrance of the aisle and cleared his throat.

Cleo turned, smiled, melted his heart, and walked toward him. "Hey," she said.

"Want some coffee?" The words were out of his mouth before he had a chance to consider the implications. To Quirk, those four syllables held a colossal amount of weight. 'Want some coffee,' in his mind, could easily be misconstrued as 'Will you marry me?'

But the fears of one are often not in the forefront of another's thoughts, and Cleo simply shook her head. "I have to get to work. Walk me there?"

Quirk's heart pitter-pattered. He would've walked across a bed of hot coals wearing gasoline-soaked shoes if she'd asked. Playing cool, he said, "Yeah, definitely. The café is too crowded anyway."

They walked through the lower level of Powell's, past the information desk, past the line of shoppers waiting to check out, up the stairs, and out the front door, pausing under the overhang. The rain had backed off, but a blanket of Portland's typical misty drizzle remained.

"Which branch?" Quirk asked, even though he already knew the answer.

"The one down on Sixth."

"You'll get soaked going back."

Cleo shrugged. "Not necessarily." She grabbed an umbrella leaning against the outer wall, smirked at him then flicked it open, stepping out onto the sidewalk.

It was risky, stealing something as innocuous as an umbrella. What if they were spotted, arrested, and questioned? A minor infraction, but that tiny butterfly beating its wings could potentially create a massive tsunami of disorder for the rest of The Clan. He and Cleo would be in the system and easily discoverable if anything went wrong after Tuesday.

What if they left traces of evidence or DNA behind? Of course, he'd look different next week. He planned to shave his beard and his head, lose the glasses and flannel, and wear a tailored suit. He'd go from Portland grunge to downtown businessman—he'd done it before and barely recognized himself—but a criminal trail left too many possibilities open.

Quirk considered snatching the umbrella away from Cleo or forcing her to return it, but...those attractive, well-toned legs, the small slit in the skirt, the way that mischievous grin beckoned him to join her when she looked back coaxed him into leaving it alone. *Forget it,* Quirk thought. I*t's just an umbrella.*

Something had changed in her demeanor, too, but he couldn't place what. Was her mood lighter? Less businesslike? Friendlier?

He pulled his skullcap on and down low, almost to his eyebrows. He shoved his hands into the pockets of his skinny jeans and followed his temptress.

A wet breeze lifted the hood of his windbreaker, reminding him that it was there. He pulled it over his head and tugged on the strings. Cleo held the umbrella higher and asked if he wanted to join her underneath it. "No," he answered, "I don't want to crowd you."

"Suit yourself. So," she said, glancing back, checking the distance between them and the nearest pedestrian, "it looked pretty standard in there, right? There's no real rhyme or reason to the shift changes and they don't have anyone patrolling the floors looking for shoplifters. Not that I could see. I mean, it's possible that they have people undercover, though I doubt it. There *could've* been, but I was focused more on looking for someone that might've been looking for us, you know? I couldn't make anybody except for this old perv trying to get a peek down my blouse."

Quirk thought about asking which one it was so that he could go back to the bookstore later and punch the guy in the face. He tucked the fantasy away and said, "It seemed like just another day in Powell's to me. I worked retail some after I got back from Iraq and more than likely the shifts are staggered so they can keep the sales floor and registers covered all the time. Regardless, it's so crowded that they won't focus on some random guy leaving a package behind on a shelf."

"But on a Tuesday morning?"

"Maybe not *as* crowded."

Cleo said, "That's the plan?"

"Technically you're not supposed to know that."

According to Boudica, each individual member of The Clan had his or her own job and had no knowledge of the other's activities. Terrorist cells operated the same way. The less you knew, the less you could implicate others and bring down the whole undertaking.

Quirk wondered why Boudica had chosen to pair him with Cleo twice, considering the fact that it violated the concept of individual cells. Two reasons came to mind; either Boudica felt Cleo—who was only twenty-four—needed some experienced guidance, or she was there to keep an eye on him. Why Moscow? Why Portland, but not Beijing or London? He didn't have an answer, and speculating would only distract him from the current job. Only Boudica knew the method to her madness.

Cleo grinned. "*Technically*, you're right. Here, hold this for a second." She handed him the umbrella.

Quirk took it and held it over her head, blocking the drizzle.

He didn't notice the handgun until he felt the barrel against his abs.

"Whoa, what's—"

Quirk was more burdened by the disappointment of having his dreams of a white picket fence with Cleo evaporate like the surrounding mist than he was with the possibility of a bullet wound.

Cleo: dream girl, love of his life, traitor.

"Quiet."

"What're you doing?"

"Shut up. Down here." She led him down a parking garage ramp, into a lower level. The bright yellow sign in the middle of the entry read "FULL," indicating a reduced risk of being spotted. No drivers entering, perhaps only a handful leaving after they'd finished shopping.

With more pressing things to focus on, Quirk forgot that he was holding the open umbrella, at least until he realized he could use it as a distraction.

Too risky, he thought. *I yank the umbrella down, she gets spooked and pulls the trigger on instinct. Gut shot, maybe I bleed out slowly behind one of these parked cars. No dice, Quirk.*

At the bottom of the ramp, Cleo turned right and Quirk followed. "Lose the umbrella," she said. He obeyed. He closed it then chucked it into the bed of a red pickup truck. Cleo backed away a step and flicked the barrel and her chin to the right. Following him between a gold minivan and a forest-green Subaru hatchback, she added, "Over there, behind that support pillar."

"Did I… Cleo, talk to me."

"Back there, out of sight."

Again, Quirk obeyed. He stopped in the shadows, behind the support pillar, and waddled underneath the ramp. It angled awkwardly overhead so that he had to stoop to fit. He lifted his hands, palms outward, and craned his neck to see her.

Cleo backed up to the post and surveyed left and right, either looking for unwanted company or witnesses, but Quirk suspected the latter. She widened her legs into a sturdier stance, screwed a silencer into the barrel, and aimed at his forehead.

"Cleo, don't," he pleaded.

"What's your real name?"

"Tell me what's going on, Cleo. Did I do something wrong? Is this because of London?"

"What's your real name?"

"Mark. Mark Ellis. Why?"

"The FBI likes to know these things."

"What?"

Cleo turned a corner of her mouth up into a half-grin. "Crime pays, but the government pays better when you're sleeping with an agent."

The burning knot in Quirk's stomach clenched tighter. "I thought you were part of the solution, not the problem. Why're you doing this?"

"Look, we all lost somebody and we all let Boudica convince us that fighting back this way was the right thing to do. Maybe it was, maybe it wasn't, but has it changed anything? No, it hasn't. And it never will. Once you realize that, there comes a time when you just have to get over it and move on."

"So your brother gets shot and your crusade only lasts a couple of years before you throw his memory away? And for what? Some peckerwood FBI guy and a few bucks?"

"They've been onto us for *two months*, Quirk, since you screwed up in London. They know everything about us. Where we live, where we work, what cars we drive. Then, about a month ago, I was cleaning underneath a nightstand in my bedroom and found some type of spy shit listening device stuck to the bottom of it. We were screwed, so as soon as he approached me with an offer, I said hell yeah. Cause or no cause, I'm not getting locked up for you people."

"And you had to sleep with him, too?" Quirk couldn't help himself. The betrayal, the jealousy—the emotions seemed childish and petty but he had to say something. It hurt, damn it. "He's what, paying you for sex and information? You're a whore. Don't you see that? Whoever this guy is, he's treating you like a whore, Cleo."

"Maybe so, but I'd rather be an FBI whore than somebody's bitch in prison."

Quirk shook his head. "Do you think you can pull that trigger?"

"I'm not supposed to kill you, moron. We're waiting."

"For what?"

"He's coming here as soon as he's done meeting with the woman you were supposed to murder."

"What're you talking about? That's not the plan."

"Cell individuality, Quirk, remember? You have no idea what the real plan was. Your job was to build your little firecracker and then make sure it went boom, right? You didn't know anything else, did you?"

"No."

"My job, not that it matters anymore, was to get this woman named Sara Winthrop into Powell's at ten o'clock next Tuesday. That's it. That's all I knew, but from what I could guess, she was on Boudica's hit list like all the rest of them."

"The rest of who?"

"The people on her list."

Confused, Quirk inched toward her.

"Step back, do *not* come any closer. On the ground, now."

Quirk dropped and felt the cold concrete through his jeans.

"Scoot back into the corner."

"Okay, okay, Jesus. I'm here." The shadows were deep and dark underneath the ramp. He shuffled farther back and felt his hand brush against something hard and loose.

"Stay there." Cleo fidgeted, looking left and right, around the edges of the support pillar. She looked anxious, as if she were wondering what was taking her FBI lover so long.

"What list, Cleo?"

"Shut up. I've told you too much already."

"Does it matter? If I'm going to prison, what does it matter that I know?"

"Maybe he'll tell you when he gets here."

"Cleo, look at me. Look. It's fine. I'm going to prison, so what, but at least tell me that all of this wasn't for nothing, that we didn't blow up all those places for some reason other than our actual agenda."

"And what was our agenda, exactly? To help the world see that video games lead to violence? It's all bullshit and you know it. Those studies prove nothing." Cleo checked her wristwatch. "Don't move. I really don't want to shoot you."

"I'm cool," he said, but he wasn't. He was far from cool. He reached to the side, pawing the concrete flooring, and found what his hand had brushed against. It was hard and jagged. Without looking away from her, he read it with his fingers, feeling a clump of cement about the size of a softball.

Cleo reached into her handbag and pulled out a cell phone. She dialed, waited, and said, "Where are you? I'm here, right now. He's not going anywhere… Well, are you coming? How long? Fine, hurry. We're too exposed. I'm afraid someone—"

A loud *kachunk* echoed throughout the lower floor as a stairway door opened nearby. It was sudden enough, and unexpected enough, to distract Cleo. Spooked and reacting on instinct, she turned toward the noise, then back to her captive. "No—"

Quirk watched as the chunk of concrete hurtled toward her in slow motion.

Perfect aim, perfect luck.

It crashed into the side of her head. The gun fired, the silencer muffling the sound as the bullet ricocheted off the ceiling and the floor.

Cleo dropped to the ground, unconscious.

Quirk scrambled to his feet and shuffled over to her, staying low behind the minivan. He picked up her handgun. It was still warm from the heat of her palm.

He aimed, choked back the regret, and fired two shots into her chest.

Then he ran.

SEVEN

Patty Kellog leaned over the coffee mug and inhaled the fresh, steaming scent. Bold, black, and strong enough for the spoon to stand up straight, just the way she liked it. She clucked her tongue and thought about how her visit here would lead to such a waste of a perfectly good explosives specialist.

She stirred the contents, ensuring the poison was mixed in well, secured the plastic lid again, and waited on Quirk and Cleo to join her in the café of Powell's. She'd spied them from a distance, climbing up and down the stairs, and as long as Cleo stuck to the plan, Quirk wouldn't be the liability she thought he was.

Patty checked the clock behind the barista counter. How much longer? Ten minutes? Fifteen? She'd told Cleo to allow him to take the lead, but if he wanted to take over an hour for their supposed "recon" mission at Powell's, then she was to convince him she was thirsty and wanted something from the café. Once there, she was to excuse herself, and then Patty—or Boudica, rather—would make her acquaintance. It would go something like, "Quirk? We haven't officially met, but I think we should talk about your…upcoming job. Here's a coffee for you. Walk with me."

Three days later, the slow-acting toxins would take their toll and The Clan would begin the process of finding a new guy that liked to make things explode.

Patty watched the entrance, getting her hopes up and being let down every time some new person walked through. Her impatience grew as she bounced a leg and checked the wall clock again.

Was it too much of a risk changing the plans like she did? Melinda Wilkes had originally been next on the list, but her sudden job transfer from Chicago to Paris left too many puzzle pieces in too many different places. She'd scrambled, reorganized, and was pleased to see that it wouldn't be too much of an effort to take care of Sara Winthrop while she still had all of her resources in the U.S.

Boudica mumbled, "Damn it, where are you?"

She stood, holding both coffees, and was so agitated that she absentmindedly took a sip from one. A brief moment of panic made her hands unsteady, and she relaxed. The coffee in her right hand, from which she'd sipped, had the small blue checkmark of safety. One more look at the clock.

A barista shouted, "Caramel latte for Amanda! Amanda?"

Boudica cursed and slung both cups into the nearest trashcan.

Cleo was fifteen minutes late. Had she told Quirk about the plan?

Something had been off with that girl for the past two months, and this had been her chance at redemption. Boudica considered the fact that maybe she should've purchased *two* coffees with room for something other than cream.

Last chance, Cleo, she thought. *If you're out, game's over.*

Patty tucked the Boudica persona away and became just another patron browsing the multitude of shelves at Powell's. She took the stairs up to the top floor and worked her way down through each level. Cleo and Quirk were nowhere to be found. Why had the girl changed her mind? Why wouldn't she deliver Quirk like she'd been asked to do? Perhaps whatever had been off about her recently had finally buried its claws deep into that shaky psyche and Cleo had been turned.

It had to be the FBI, and Cleo had to be The Clan's leak.

Six months ago, when Boudica and the others had discovered that the FBI was closing in on their little operation, they had begun deliberately feeding them false information. Creating fake accounts, fake conversations, fake trails that had been manipulated to look legitimate, all the way back to before that first explosion in Moscow. They concocted a whole storyline, and from what she could tell, it had worked, up to a point.

The gambit with Chicago had been risky, blatantly leaking information about their next target, daring the Feds to catch them. The plan was to let the day pass, allow them to feel like they'd been successful in its prevention then strike when the threat no longer appeared credible.

And then Melinda had moved. Change of internal plans, but they kept the ruse going in the underground, smoke-filled caves of the hidden internet. The play was supposedly still on. The actual target was gone, but the FBI wasn't aware of it. From what they suspected to be true, the CBOE was the next location on The Clan's list.

It was perfect, actually. They'd have all their attention directed toward Chicago while The Clan slipped quietly away to their new objective in Portland.

Finish the job in the Rose City, escape to Paris where Melinda would be eliminated, and then quietly purge the remaining members of The Clan. No traces, no trails, no way of ever revealing who'd been a part of the group that had caused so much chaos around the world.

Boudica learned through Chief, her man on the inside, that the FBI had uncovered the truth behind the new plan for Portland, but hadn't officially let on in their communications. From what she'd gathered, the FBI's ploy was to leave a task force in Chicago, as if they were still waiting on things to proceed as intended, and then send a smaller team to Portland to intercept them.

She'd traced and retraced every single step The Clan had made for the past couple of months, trying to find out where and how they'd screwed up. There were no missteps whatsoever. She was painstaking in her review and didn't sleep for two days. They were clean. There had been no mistakes.

Which could only mean one thing. Someone in their group had betrayed them.

Originally, she'd suspected Quirk. After things hadn't gone as planned in London, she'd ridden him hard, perhaps too hard, and maybe it'd been too much. He seemed to be the most likely culprit, the easiest choice. Cleo was off, too, but it hadn't made Boudica suspicious enough to waste the young woman's talents as a thief and forger.

Not until today. If Cleo had revealed the truth to Quirk—whether it was regarding Boudica's plans to dispose of him or whether she'd made it known that she was an FBI informant—now there would be two problems that needed solving.

The question was, where were they?

Boudica left Powell's and headed up the street with no particular destination in mind—at least not until she'd determined where her two miscreants had gone. She removed her disposable cell from her handbag and dialed a number she'd only had to use once before.

When he answered, Boudica said, "Spirit?"

"Yes."

"Were you able to get that tracking chip into Cleo's burner?"

"I don't know what that is." His voice was flat and sterile. The Spirit was an ancient ex-KGB agent—a relic from the Cold War, tossed aside when newer, faster, younger recruits were brought in. He was old back then. Now he didn't just have one foot in the grave, he was standing with the grass at waist level.

However, he hadn't lost his touch, and from what Boudica had heard before she hired him, he was as proficient as he had been in 1983. The Spirit had certainly performed quality work when it came time to take care of Alvarez.

"Her *burner*. The disposable cell phone she had. You know, the thing where you push a few buttons, it goes *beep-beep-beep* and sends a signal up into outer space and then you get to talk to somebody else?"

"Yes. Of course."

"Did you or did you not get the tracking chip installed?"

"Dimitri says it is so."

"Good. Where is she?"

"One moment."

Boudica listened to him bark instructions in Russian, and then heard a keyboard clattering in the background. It was risky allowing him to work with a partner, because there was always too many variables exposed, but he needed help with the current technology. The Spirit was an old-school, cloak-and-dagger agent, used to working in shadows and lies, too outdated to learn new tricks. His philosophy was why bother wasting the time when he might die in his sleep that night? Boudica suspected that if she were to hand him an iPod, he wouldn't know what to do with it.

She waited, growing impatient, as the Spirit and his partner muttered to themselves in the background. "Anything?"

He coughed into the receiver. "She's in a parking garage. Downtown Portland."

"Really? Where?" He gave her the address. "That's two blocks from here. Is she on the move?"

"No, she's stationary."

"How long has she been there?" Boudica asked. "Maybe I can catch her."

The Spirit mumbled something in Russian. It sounded like he was speaking around a mouthful of marbles, drunk on cheap potato vodka. "Tracking software says… Dimitri? Dimitri says two minutes. Two minutes, no movement."

Boudica hung up, used her sleeves to wipe the disposable phone free of prints, snapped it in half, and then dropped it into a nearby recycling container.

She cut left across the street, walking fast and hoping she would make it to the parking garage in time to catch Cleo. She readjusted her handbag on her shoulder and felt the weight of her compact 9mm shifting inside.

EIGHT

Sara leaned forward in her seat and pointed at the whiteboard. She said, "You're kidding me, right?"

Timms shook his head. "No, ma'am."

Sara almost laughed. "Little Patty Kellog is this *Boudica* person? She's the leader of some group of international terrorists?"

"Yes."

"There's no way."

"Why not?"

"There's absolutely no way that the timid, goofy girl who grew up down the street from me is behind all this. It's not possible. I went to high school with her, for God's sake."

Timms shrugged. "I graduated with Michael Jordan. What's your point?"

Teddy, who'd apparently grown bored with the conversation that didn't revolve around him, perked up. "Whoa, Michael Jordan? Is that true?"

"I sat behind him in algebra."

"Cool."

"It is *now*, yeah, but the point I'm trying to make to *you*," he said, turning to Sara, "is that it's not *probable* that people from our past can become what they are, but it's not *impossible*. Honestly, I never thought Mike's jump shot was all that great."

Jim tapped a finger on his desk. "Agent Timms, is this going anywhere?"

Barker agreed, adding, "Who, where, what, and why, Timms. Get on with it."

"You want the shortened version?"

"That would've been nice an hour ago."

Timms grabbed a red marker, popped the top off, and wrote, "SARA WINTHROP" in big, bold letters. He underlined her name twice and then circled it. "There's your target."

Sara swallowed hard with a mixture of disbelief and fear. This seriously couldn't be happening again, could it? She felt lightheaded and confused. "*Me*? Why?"

"We're piecing that together. Do the names Melinda Wilkes, Julie Harland, Rebecca Carter, Lucy Marris, and Colleen Bishop mean anything to you?"

The muddled images in Sara's mind, like an out-of-focus photograph from the past, slowly began to sharpen. Dull forms became recognizable objects. She could see the shapes of realization gaining some clarity. Perturbed, she said, "If you know those names, then you already know they mean something to me."

"Yes, but what?"

"We all graduated together and we sort of have...something."

"I'm aware. In part, at least."

"If you know all of this, then why—oh God, are they targets, too?"

"*Were* targets. Four of them are already dead, Mrs. Winthrop."

"No." The word slipped softly from her lips. She hadn't been friends with them—not exactly—but they'd been the upper-echelon clique that Sara had so desperately wanted to be a part of all those years ago. It sat heavy on her heart knowing those women were now gone.

She was surprised she hadn't heard anything about it from friends or family, but she'd long ago given up Facebook, and in a metro area the size of northern Virginia, where she had grown up, people disappeared easily among the masses. She hadn't spoken to some of her classmates in over twenty years and hadn't bothered with the latest reunion.

Timms crossed his arms and moved closer to Sara. Barker kept his legs extended as a barrier. Timms stopped but didn't step over them. "All true, I'm afraid. Julie Harland was on vacation in Moscow. Rebecca Carter taught English classes in Beijing. Lucy

Marris was a fashion photographer on assignment in Rio. And Colleen Bishop was in London for her great-grandfather's funeral."

"What about Melinda?"

"We believe she was the intended target in Chicago."

"Are you protecting her?"

"From a distance. She's in Paris."

Barker scoffed, "That's quite the distance."

"We have a team on the ground there. She'll be fine."

Sara said, "I don't understand. I thought you said that all these bombings were tied to video game violence."

"They are, in an approximate way, and I'll explain all of that in a minute, but from what we know, it was a cover-up for the real mission objectives. So what I want to know, Mrs. Winthrop, is how the six of you women are connected to Patty Kellog other than the fact that you all went to the same high school."

"How did you learn about that?"

"Standard procedure. We cross-referenced all the victims to see if they had anything in common."

"Right." Sara stood and went to the window, staring down to the street three stories below. With her back turned to them, partly in shame, partly in regret, she said, "It was the homecoming football game—"

Timms's cell phone chimed on his belt clip and he said, "Hold that thought, Mrs. Winthrop." He checked the caller ID. "Yeah, I need to take this." He stepped to a far corner of the office. He kept his voice low, but not low enough to hide his side of the conversation. "What? I'm at LightPulse. Are you in the nest yet? Is he secure? Good… I'll be there. Two minutes, tops. What was that noise? Emily? Emily? Answer me."

Timms turned back to face the room with everyone focused intently on him. His eyes were wide. His left hand shook as he tugged an earlobe. "That was…a colleague of mine. I should've been gone five minutes ago. Listen to me. You all need to do exactly what I say, because there's no time for questions—"

Teddy being, well, *Teddy*, interrupted him. "Who was that?"

Timms inhaled deeply. It didn't change the bright red color of his cheeks. "We're in play. I don't know what just happened, but I need all of you to listen. Mr. Rutherford, sir, you and Teddy—LightPulse—you're free and clear. Go home, stay safe, and cover for Sara on Monday morning."

Sara said, "Cover for me? What does—"

Teddy held his hands up. "Whoa, *no*, wait. Don't shove me out of this."

Timms scrambled over to Karen Wallace. "Can you help?"

Nodding, Karen said, "I'm all yours."

Timms rubbed his face. "Do you still have friends in the FBI?"

"A few."

"Okay, here's what I need. Use whatever connections you still have, okay? I'd put in some calls for you but I don't have the time. What I need is for you to try to find a man named Vadim Bariskov."

"The *Spirit*?"

Clearly her knowledge surprised Timms. "You know Bariskov?"

"Stories, that's all."

"Find him if you can. We think he's still in Portland. Last known movement, as of this morning, was a rental car that visited the Rose Gardens. White sedan. He was with his partner. He may still be there, he may not."

Sara shivered at the memories. The first level of Shelley Sergeant's game had been to stand nude among the roses, being humiliated while onlookers gawked and pointed.

"On it." Karen stood. "What happens when we find him?"

"Monitor him, nothing more. Do not engage, but

absolutely do not lose him. I'll be in touch."

"Maybe easier said than done."

Teddy said, "I can help. Karen, seriously, let me come with you."

Karen rolled her eyes, looked to Jim for approval, and through some miracle on Teddy's desperate, puppy-dog behalf, she relented. "Stay out of the way." Karen left the office, and Teddy floated out behind her on smiles and imaginary rainbows.

Timms said, "Barker, I want you to take Mrs. Winthrop back to her house. Don't rush, don't act panicked in case her home is under Clan surveillance that we haven't picked up on yet, but get her and the children out of there and to a safe place. Listen to me: that's imperative, okay? We need to keep this trap alive as long as we can. Mrs. Winthrop, we have people on your street and they would've alerted me to any activity, so your family is safe. Don't worry, don't panic, just get them out of there. Let me know when you're secure. And Barker, no matter what, keep her protected."

"Done," Barker agreed.

Timms shook his hand in a show of genuine concern, grabbed his suit jacket, and darted out the door.

The silence in the room was overbearing as Jim,

Sara, and Barker all stared at each other in the wake of such frantic, hasty exits. Sara said to Barker, "Should we go?"

"Get your coat. Mr. Rutherford, you'll be okay?"

"Always, Detective. If you need a place, my house has a panic room."

"Thank you, Jim," Sara said.

"You're welcome, now *go*."

***

Sara slammed the unmarked sedan's door closed and latched her seatbelt.

How could something like this be happening again? She couldn't believe it, couldn't wrap her mind around it. It was unfathomable.

"You really think they're safe, like he said?"

"Cops and Feds mix about as well as oil and water, but yeah, I believe him."

"Jesus. Can we hurry without acting like we know something's up?"

Barker tried to relieve her tension. "You're a hot mess, you know that?" He chuckled and playfully patted her shoulder. Barker started the car, whipped it out of the parking space, and then launched into the stream of traffic.

“I can't take much more of this.” Sara pinched the bridge of her nose. She practiced breathing as he drove, counting her patterns, relaxing, relaxing. “Can I ask you something?”

“Go for it.”

"I'm a good soul, right?"

"Of course. Why?"

“I don't know. These past couple of years, it just seems like trouble is looking for me on purpose. Whom did I piss off for that to happen?"

"Well, if the universe ain't on your side, you’ve got me, at least."

“Thanks.” Sara smiled. “Still doesn’t explain why.”

“I don’t know. Does ‘shit happens’ work as an explanation?”

“Not in the slightest.”

The traffic moved well for a Saturday morning, but not well enough. He almost turned on his police lights then pulled his hand away. Like Timms had said, if they were under Clan surveillance, it might alert them that something was wrong and would put Sara’s children, and Miss Willow, in danger. In fact, he realized, he probably shouldn’t have peeled out of the parking lot like he had.

Sara said, “Can’t you go faster?”

“Not if we want to keep the cover on. If they’re

watching, they'll know. Best bet is to play it cool and stay calm. Don't forget, Timms said he had people watching your place. They're safe."

Sara shook her head and leaned against the door. She put a shaky hand on her forehead, sheltering her eyes. "How am I supposed to stay calm when somebody wants to kill me *again*?"

"I know, I'm sorry, but it's—"

"Do you? Do you know?"

"Sara, I'm a cop. I wake up every day wondering if any number of guys I put away twenty years ago will show up on my doorstep the moment they get out of prison, so yeah, I know what it's like."

"I'm—yeah, sorry. It's just that—I mean, my God, why me?"

"It's like you're getting picked for jury duty over and over again." Barker signaled, checked his mirrors, and ducked into the left lane. He found a gap in traffic and turned into a residential neighborhood where the traffic was lighter.

Sara tried to calm herself with a joke. "Jury duty? I'll take the death threats." She looked around at the familiar homes. She passed this area every weekday on her way into the office, and she thought back to the day she found the note on her minivan. It wasn't far from here that she'd sped through another neighborhood, nearly catching air off of speed bumps in a mad rush to get to Jacob's school. It was almost as if fate, or coincidence, were unintentionally recreating the scene.

She called home and when Miss Willow answered, she was relieved to learn that the kids were fine, happily eating snacks and watching *Cars* for the five hundredth time that week. Sara offered little in the way of details, but insisted that Miss Willow get herself and the children ready to leave for a few days.

Barker listened to her say, "I'll explain when we get there, just pack their overnight bags. Yeah, you should probably come with us… We're hoping for fifteen minutes. Twenty at the most."

When Sara hung up, he asked, "Freak her out?"

"Not really. She's so calm. Thank God she's been around the house since they put Shelley away, because she's been my rock, for sure."

Barker honked his horn at a jogger who'd drifted dangerously close to the center of the street. The guy jumped, pulled an earbud from his left ear, waved, and then moved over to the sidewalk. "Idiot," Barker said. "These people running around here with their iPads and the music turned up too loud."

Sara chuckled. "They're called iPods. An iPad is like an oversized iPhone."

"How about this? *I* don't care."

"*Sure* you don't."

"Do you use that Twitter thing with an iPod?"

"You're joking, right?"

Barker grinned. "I got a smile out of you, at least. Relax, Sara, we'll be fine. We'll get you and the kids and Willow somewhere safe, you'll camp out for a few days until we're all clear, then you'll go back to normal."

Sara leaned back into the car seat and pulled her jacket tighter around her chest. "What's normal these days? Our lives in danger? More death threats?"

"This'll be the last one, I promise."

"I hope you're right."

"I know I'm right. And besides, I may bust the dude's chops a little bit, but I can tell Timms knows what he's doing, so take some deep breaths and try to be calm. I'm not trying to patronize you, because you know the deal, but have some faith in the system. Unlike that business with the Sergeant girl, we're ahead of the game this time."

"Really?" she said.

"What?"

"Ahead of *the game*? Pun intended?"

"What? Uh—right. Sorry. That was…punintentional. Get it? Pun and unintentional?"

"Oh, I get it."

Barker chuckled. "Everything will be okay, Sara. Trust me."

She nodded without believing it. "Okay."

"Now, do you mind telling me what in the hell you did to this Kellog woman twenty years ago?"

Sara laid her head back against the headrest and closed her eyes. She didn't want to remember. She'd tried so hard to forget.

NINE

Patty Kellog gently opened the heavy metal door in the northeastern corner of the parking garage, trying to prevent any echoing noise. She tiptoed into the lower level, peeking left and right, looking for Cleo…and maybe Quirk. Chances were if Cleo had informed Quirk of the plan to poison him the guy was long gone. But why was Cleo here in the parking garage, not moving?

It made no sense. According to the Spirit she'd been stationary for two minutes, and it had taken Patty at least five to speedwalk here. She'd dialed him again with a spare disposable phone, learned that Cleo hadn't moved, and again tossed the device in the trash.

Was Cleo on the phone with the FBI, spilling details of The Clan's operations? Was that why she hadn't moved? No, she'd likely done that already, plus, the FBI wouldn't risk leaving her alone. They'd pick her up, bring her in, and ask questions in the comfort of an interrogation room.

Was she sitting in a car with Quirk, revealing particulars? That didn't work, either. She could've explained everything necessary on the walk here from Powell's.

Next best guess was…Cleo was dead. She'd told Quirk, he'd led her away, and then he'd murdered her in the seclusion of the parked cars. It was quiet down below. Plenty of cars, trucks, and vans for cover. Secluded and convenient.

Until the door slammed behind her. The *kachunk* reverberated around the walls. Patty jumped, cursed, and ducked behind a blue Jeep Wrangler. She listened for the sound of a starting car, but what followed instead surprised her.

That unmistakable sound.

The chuff of a bullet through a silencer not too far away.

A thump that sounded like a mass falling against the side of a car.

And then two more muffled pops.

Patty tried to piece it together in her mind. The sound of the door shutting had surprised someone. The first shot was possibly a reaction to the distraction. The dull sound of something falling against a vehicle—a body falling—was it Cleo? Was it Quirk? Then, the two additional pops.

Chuff-chuff through the silencer.

A double-tap to the chest. Had to be.

Who was it? Cleo had been stationary for so long. Had Quirk taken her captive, demanding answers? Possibly. Three shots total. The double-tap was a decisive end, so at least one of her two problems were taken care of, and she hoped that the first shot, the reaction to the door's noise, hadn't gone errant of its target.

She had her answer—and it wasn't the one she wanted—when Quirk rounded the lower corner and sprinted up the western ramp.

Patty hesitated, trying to decide what came next. He was fast. He'd be up the ramp and onto the streets before she could catch up, if she could catch up at all. Taking care of him in broad daylight would be messy, dangerous, and stupid. There were cameras everywhere these days. Outside of shops, in ATMs, on streetlights. She'd be easily identifiable. She'd taken a big risk merely by walking the streets of Portland that morning.

The police, the FBI—whoever had access to the video surveillance tapes—could trace her movements in reverse, and who knew how far. Maybe even back to the safe house if they were able to track the route she'd driven through traffic cams.

She cursed and let him go. A couple of phone calls…he wouldn't get that far.

She stood up, checked the parking lot for any

additional witnesses, and seeing none, she jogged in the direction from which Quirk had come. She paused at the western ramp and looked up, ensuring he was out of sight, and continued.

Moving in a crouch from car to car, inspecting the space between each of them, she finally found what she was looking for about twenty yards away, closer to the eastern entrance.

Cleo lay between a minivan and a green Subaru. Face up, eyes lifeless, with two bullet holes in the center of her chest.

In a way, Patty was disappointed, because one, she would've enjoyed taking care of Cleo herself, and two, she also wouldn't have the privilege of torturing her for more information. Questions like what had she told Quirk? Was she working for the FBI officially? How much did they know? And if she had turned traitor, had she told Sara Winthrop the truth about Patty's identity already? That would be unfortunate and make the situation difficult, but not impossible. Problems could easily be surpassed as long as you knew whom to pay.

Patty stared at the blood on Cleo's white top. If she looked at it from the right angle, the blotting looked like a pair of butterfly wings. It was almost pretty.

She needed to move. Now. Security cameras had likely captured Quirk and Cleo entering, and then Patty entering not long after. They would have video evidence of Quirk leaving, but not Cleo.

What to do, what to do? she thought. *Steal a car?*

Was that the best option? Perhaps not. The owner would report it stolen. The police would have verifiable video evidence. At some point, they would put the sequences together and the footage might show up in the media with a byline such as, "Authorities seek man in blue windbreaker and woman in white jacket as possible murder suspects."

Patty shook her head and put her hands on her hips. "Shit." She knew she should've thought it through, but she'd been so frustrated and intent on finding Cleo that she hadn't assessed the ramifications of being out in the open. However, there had been no way of knowing that Quirk would murder Cleo and leave her in a bind. She'd now become a suspect merely by circumstance. She ran her fingers through her hair and backed away from Cleo's body.

The sounds of hurried footsteps caught her attention. She glanced to the right.

A man in a dark blue suit with a matching tie ran toward her. He looked official. Authoritative. His face seemed familiar, like perhaps they'd crossed paths recently, or perhaps she'd seen a picture of—Jesus, it was Donald Timms. FBI. The agent that her informant had warned her about, the one that had gotten too close.

Think, Patty. Think.

She screamed, "Over here, hurry! Oh my God, she's been shot. Somebody shot this woman!"

He shouted back, "Is she alive? Is she?" as his footsteps pounded, descending the ramp. He pulled his firearm from its holster. "Stay right there. Don't move. Answer me, is she alive?"

Patty held up her hands. "I don't know. I can't tell. I don't think so."

"Did you see anything?"

"No."

Timms reached her, sweating and pale. He looked down at Cleo's body.

Patty watched his face. She saw a flicker of pain and regret flash in his expression and then he returned to stoic business. "Ma'am," he said, showing his ID, "Agent Timms with the FBI—do you have a cell phone?"

"No, no, I don't."

He unclipped his from his belt holster and dialed a number, then tried to keep one eye on Patty while he kneeled to examine Cleo's body. He said into the phone, "It's Timms. Confirmed. Cleo is down, repeat, Cleo is down. No pulse. Get them here, now. I don't know the exact address, hang on." Timms turned to face her. "What's the address here?"

Patty forced her bottom lip to quiver, pretending. "I don't know."

"What street are we on?"

"I don't know, I can't think! Sixth, maybe?"

"Sixth and something," he said into the phone. "There's a furniture store across from us. Just get here." He flicked a look over his shoulder at Patty and lowered the gun. "Did you hear anything? See anything? Was she with anyone?"

"I found her like that, I swear. Please don't—I was just trying to get to my car, and, and…" Patty forced herself into mock panic and shortened breaths. She fanned her face and stumbled.

"Okay, okay, I believe you. You're not in any trouble."

Timms turned away from her and focused on Cleo.

Wait, Patty thought, *he called her Cleo. He knows. He definitely knows.*

He bent over, examining the wounds in her chest.

Patty moved without a sound.

Timms froze as Patty pressed the silencer of her

9mm against his skull just behind his left ear. "Fuck. Boudica?" he said.

"Nice meeting you in person, Timms."

"Somebody's had some work done."

"The best cheekbones money can buy."

She squeezed the trigger. Red sprayed onto Cleo's white shirt as Timms fell on top of her.

Patty tucked the gun into her handbag and tried to decide what to do next. Avoiding any security cameras was imperative. She removed her jacket, thought about throwing it out, and then put it back on again. On a normal day, a jacket in a trashcan would hardly arouse suspicion, but with two dead bodies, one of them a Federal agent's, and the possibility of her image on the surveillance tapes, they would take the jacket as evidence, run DNA tests, and she'd be made.

She'd spent a lot of money trying to have her identity erased physically and electronically along with every paper trail imaginable, but one could never be sure what potential problems were out there.

Patty turned and went back to the stairwell where she'd descended earlier. She pulled on a pair of gloves, opened the door, wiped the interior handle, and then took the stairs in twos. At the ground level floor, she scanned the area around her, looking for people near their cars, and seeing none, she ran straight, slipping between a Suburban and a white Volkswagen Beetle. With a slight jump, she landed on top of the dividing wall, slung her legs across, and then dropped to the sidewalk.

An elderly gentleman walking a large Greyhound startled her. Smiling, he said, "I wish I was still that limber," and continued past. Patty paused, hesitated with her hand around the 9mm's grip, and then decided to let him live. She hoped it wouldn't cost her.

She walked briskly, with her head down, into the rain.

With Timms and Cleo eliminated, two of her potential problems were gone. The fact that Timms was now dead wouldn't stop the FBI, however, and it was simply a matter of how long before the next in line would take his place in resuming the hunt for The Clan. Conservatively, it could take them twelve hours to get up to speed, but more than likely it would be a lot less. So much depended on how good Timms had been about sharing information. The reports she'd gotten suggested he was a loner and a bit of a maverick, so there was a chance that providence was on her side.

Patty muttered, "Now what?" and kept walking. She took her jacket off, turned it inside out, and put it back on, blue side out. She pulled a baby blue knitted cap from her bag and tugged it over her head. The police and the Feds wouldn't be anywhere near searching for a blonde woman in a white jacket yet, but her minimal disguise might prevent the other pedestrians from identifying her later.

If Timms knew Cleo by her codename, Patty thought, *and recognized me by mine, then he definitely had inside information on the Sara Winthrop objective.*

If that was true, where was she now?

Every bit of information has a price, Sara. It won't be long.

However, finding Quirk was the next logical step. What did he know? What had Cleo told him? And why had he murdered her?

By the time she made it to her car back in the Powell's parking garage, she was thoroughly drenched and annoyed. She hated Portland, mostly because of the weather. Sun, drizzle, pouring rain, all in a five-minute span. Rinse and repeat. She longed for the somewhat stable climate of northern Virginia where she had grown up. At least there, the four distinct seasons gave you some kind of warning.

She got into her rental—a small, four-door Chevrolet—started the engine, and waited on the heater to warm up as she plotted her next move.

If I were Quirk, where would I go? God, too many places to count.

"Come on, warm up already." She slapped the vent, pointing the chilly air away from her face.

She took her third disposable phone of the day from the glove box and called the Spirit again.

"Yes?"

"It's me. Yesterday you said that was a negative on Quirk's tracer, right?"

"Unfortunately, yes. He never left his home and Dimitri was unable to—"

"Never mind. It's too late now, anyway. That little wench Cleo was the leak."

"Would you like me to…take out the trash?"

"No need. Quirk did it for us. Timms is out of play, too."

"Interesting."

"Yeah." Patty sighed and watched a young couple, maybe in their late twenties, as they pushed a stroller over to their minivan. Some days, she thought a normal life would've been nice. Possibilities were just that…possible. She said, "We might have a little snag."

"Why is this?"

"There's a chance that Cleo leaked our plans to Quirk, too, and I need to find him before he can turn himself in and cut a deal."

"Indeed. I would think so."

"I have no idea where he could've gone. Any

ideas?" She listened to the old Russian breathing heavily into the receiver.

He said, "Considering the fact that there's exotic explosive material in his basement—a bomb with his fingerprints all over it—if it were me, I'd go home first. Of course, he could conceivably go to the nearest FBI office, but it's been my experience that the first natural reaction is to cover the trails you've left behind."

Patty smiled. "Makes sense to me. Good thinking."

"Boudica?"

"What?"

"Do what you must, but think twice before you waste unparalleled talent."

"Yeah, well, that depends on what he knows or whom he's going to tell. Let's…"

"Yes?"

"Let's get Plan B moving."

"I'm not sure that's the—"

"Plan B." Patty hung up, started the car, and programmed the GPS for directions to Quirk's home.

TEN

By the third stoplight, Karen Wallace had already thought of six ways she could get rid of Teddy Rutherford, and nearly all of them involved time in prison as a consequence. She'd agreed to let him come along because his father paid well and she couldn't risk losing her only steady client.

Going out on her own *was* quite lucrative, when she was able to find the proper work, but occasionally she longed for the security of a stable job.

Maybe once the dust settled with this case, she'd have a sit-down with Donald Timms and pick his brain about the current state of affairs back in the FBI offices. She'd been nudged out after threatening a sexual harassment lawsuit against one of her superiors, and according to her exit handler, she was wise to take the severance.

The *bribe.*

She'd had a solid case and knew she would've caused some serious waves, but she wouldn't have won, no matter how clear-cut the details were.

So she'd gotten as far away as possible, used the money to start her own private investigation service, and, like Sara had told her numerous times, she'd left behind one harassment lawsuit to encounter one waiting to happen in the form of Teddy Rutherford.

He was harmless, more or less, but goddamn annoying no matter how you looked at it. The guy didn't understand the word no. Dealing with Teddy was like trying to train a puppy not to shit on the carpet, but no matter how many times you shoved his nose in the pile of crap, he just didn't get it.

Thankfully, her interactions with him were few and far between. Jim had her come into the office a couple of times per month to brief him on routine checks regarding Sara's life outside of work. Was anyone following her? No. Was the security system on her house fully functional? Yes. Did you replace the batteries in the—yes, yes, and yes.

The same questions, every second and fourth Tuesday.

The same parrying of Teddy's advances, every second and fourth Tuesday.

In the passenger's seat, taking up valuable oxygen, was Teddy, fidgeting and unable to stop talking long enough for her to think. He turned the radio dial, changing the station from the soft classical that Karen preferred. She slapped his hand away and pushed a preset channel button, returning the channel to the proper station. A piece by Chopin lilted through the car as Teddy rubbed his hand and said, "You *want* to listen to this?"

Karen clenched her teeth together, molar grinding molar. "Yes. My car, my radio. I'm sorry if classical is too highbrow for you."

"No, I mean, I'm cool with it…it's just that Chopin was too much of a sissy. He didn't really attack the composition the way he could've, you know? Whenever I listen to him, I picture the guy holding a tiny cupcake and drinking tea with his pinkie held out."

Dumbfounded, Karen said, "I'm sorry, what did you just say?"

"Chopin…he's a weakling. If I'm going to invest my time in a composer, I want the guy eating a raw steak with his bare hands. I don't want him…I don't know, *dainty*, I guess."

Karen couldn't stop herself from smiling. "Okay, who are you and what have you done with Teddy Rutherford?"

"Huh?"

"Nothing, never mind. I have some CDs there in the center console. Whom would you prefer? Beethoven?"

"*Pffft*. That old queen?"

One animated double take later, Karen asked,

"You're kidding, right?"

Teddy laughed. "Yeah. Beethoven's fine," he said, pulling out the zipped-up case of CDs. As he flipped through them, he asked, "So that's crazy about Sara, huh?"

"That poor woman has been through way too much already. Her husband disappeared and was murdered, that insane girl kidnapped her kids and made her play that horrible game, and now this? These past three or four years have been trying for her. I don't know how she seems so…"

"Stable?"

"I was going to say 'together,' but stable works, too."

"There's a difference between seeming and being." Teddy slipped a Beethoven collection into the CD player. He said, "The Fifth or the Seventh?"

"Seventh," Karen answered. She checked her mirrors and merged onto the entrance ramp for I-5.

"Good choice." Teddy adjusted the volume to a reasonable level and asked, "Sara's strong, man. After that game she played, I started calling her Badass Chick. She's the B.C. Saved my life."

"I'm aware, Teddy." She was curious about Teddy's experience in the cabin, but she didn't have time for the distraction. Finding Vadim Bariskov had to be at the forefront of her thoughts.

"And what was up with meeting in that empty office, huh? Did you do weird shit like that when you were in the FBI? What was the point?"

"Total guess, but it sounded like he needed to be in the vicinity of something."

"Like what?"

"You heard him. Wherever he needed to be was nearby because he said he could be there in two minutes. Maybe he was just trying to juggle too much at once."

"He seemed pretty freaked out when he left," Teddy said. He stayed silent for a while, watching the windshield wipers swish back and forth. "I should probably tell you that we think you're doing a great job before I bring this up, so, yeah, you're doing awesome, but can I ask you something?"

"And…here it comes." Karen slipped her car between a limousine and a logging truck like a sheet of paper between the building blocks of the Great Pyramid.

"What's coming?"

"I think I know what you're going to say."

Teddy felt his right hand cramping then realized his knuckles had gone white as his fingers wrapped around the door handle. If he'd known Karen drove this poorly, he might've reconsidered his courtship ritual. "So Dad…uh, I mean *Jim* is paying you to have Sara's back, right? I'm not…I mean, man, I think you're fantastic, I really do, but—"

"How'd I miss this?"

"Yeah. You get paid to be one hundred percent on top of Sara, looking out for her."

"I'm surprised no one asked me back in that office. Believe me, I was sitting there gnawing on the inside of my cheek the whole time just waiting for it, and dreading it if it did come up, because honestly, I don't have an answer."

Teddy studied her for a moment, allowing his crush to resurface. He admired her long neck. Graceful fingers. High cheekbones. She was everything he wasn't. Tall, attractive, thin. She had angles. He was round. He'd gained weight since encountering the darker side of humanity. He blamed the dreams.

People liked Karen. He adored her. He didn't want to accuse her of shoddy work. Crush or no crush—infatuation in its purest form—Sara and her children were honorary members of the Rutherford family, and if it meant firing this beautiful angel that drove like a drunk Dario Franchitti at the Indy 500, then so be it, if it came to that.

Teddy turned the radio off. Beethoven could wait.

"How could you *not* have an answer, Karen? You've practically lived inside Sara's head for the past year and a half. How does something this big slip past you?"

Karen pursed her lips and tapped an index finger on the steering wheel. "I don't know. I've looked at every bit of her history, her present, and her future—anything that I could find that would possibly indicate the potential for trouble. She gave me full access. Said her children and their safety were more important than her privacy. I missed it. God, I don't know how, but I missed it. This Patricia Kellog, she wasn't even on the radar. It had to have been something that Sara kept hidden from me."

"She's always been private," Teddy agreed, "but after that craziness with Shelley, she wrapped this sort of…emotional *shroud* around herself for the longest time. She put on a good show, but seriously, I mean, we were worried about her. Like, her sanity." He leaned over and lowered his voice, as if someone were eavesdropping. "Don't you dare tell her I said this, but that was part of the reason I started calling her 'Badass Chick.' She needed the confidence boost."

"I'm sure she appreciated it."

"Maybe. The genesis of the whole thing was when Brian disappeared, but she held up really well for those two years. After Shelley, though, man, she tried to put up a good front and it took my dad about three months before he was able to convince her we needed to hire someone like you."

Karen nodded and changed lanes without looking. Teddy winced. She said, "Yeah, those first few rounds of interviews didn't go that well—you know, where I was trying to dig into her background. She admitted later that she didn't feel like she needed me there and definitely didn't *want* me there. Totally pulling the badass routine on me. Then I showed up one Saturday morning—Miss Willow was out with the kids somewhere—and I found Sara on her couch, wrapped up in a blanket and crying into a cup of coffee and bourbon."

"What happened?"

"Nightmare about her kids being back in the boxes again, only this time she didn't solve the puzzle in time."

"Harsh."

"Yeah. That's when she opened up."

"But never anything about Patty Kellog?"

"Not a word."

"What if we go looking for her instead of this Russian dude? She's the leader, right? She's the one with the grudge who wants to kill Sara, so why in the hell are we looking for Baryshnikov?"

"Vadim Bariskov."

"Same thing."

"If you say so."

"I'm serious."

"No, Patty Kellog and whatever happens with her is up to Timms. He's good, he's got the manpower he needs, and he'll be on top of it. If we find Bariskov and keep an eye on him, he might lead us to her anyway."

"Fine." Teddy crossed his arms and leaned against the door, staring out the window.

"I know you're worried about her, but seriously, our job is just as important."

"Okay."

Karen actually signaled, gave a quick peek over her shoulder, cut across two lanes of traffic, and barreled down the exit ramp.

Once he'd released his death grip on the door handle and could breathe properly, Teddy asked, "Where are we going?"

"To look for Bariskov."

"I know that, Karen—*where* are we looking?"

"A couple of spots I know of. Places where the Russian immigrants like to hang out."

"Like what?"

"Churches. A local market."

Teddy shrugged. "Your call."

"You have a better idea?"

"We can go to those places if you really don't want to find Bariskov."

Karen waffled between reminding him who was the actual private detective and to shut the hell up. She decided to let him speak, give his opinion, and *then* put him in his place. "Okay, hotshot," she said. "Where do you suggest?"

"There's a bar downtown called Firebrand. There's a backroom poker game going on there twenty-four hours a day. Bunch of ex-Russian mafia guys who basically sit around and pass the same thousand bucks through the pot all day long, or until some poor sucker gets invited to the game and they take everything he has."

"Bullshit. Seriously?"

"Why would I make that up?"

"How do you know about this?"

"Maybe three years ago…yeah, actually, I remember it was back in 2010, we'd started development on this game called *Red Mob*—"

"You were designing a game based on the Russian mafia?"

"*Were*, yeah. Anyway, my dad wanted me to do some field research or whatever to help this kid Jeremy with writing the plot line and backstory."

"*You*?"

"I know, right?" Teddy chuckled. "It was probably easier than writing me out of his will. It took me a few days of going to the worst bars I could find, staying out all night, asking questions, playing nice with these godawful East European hookers—"

"Right, you *had* to do that."

"No, I'm serious. You would've been proud, because my detective skills were awesome. There was this one blonde girl, maybe twenty-one at the most, who had the most amazing set of…whoa, you know, that's not important—"

"Thank you."

"Right. Her name was Irina and after I'd bought her a few drinks, I started asking around because she…I don't know, she just looked like she'd seen the wrong side of the tracks. Turns out, all it took was for me to get about five shots of vodka in her and she wouldn't shut up. Two minutes of asking questions, suddenly I've got the hookup that I've been looking for. Irina's grandfather was this big-time arms dealer back in the early eighties and was something like a general in the Russian mob. When I told her what I was doing for LightPulse, she practically dragged me into the poker room."

"No way."

"I was scared shitless, to be honest. There were maybe be six guys there, like, these big, massive Russian guys, all smoking cigars and wearing tracksuits. Super-stereotypes. I guess you could picture Malkovich in *Rounders* as Teddy KGB. Actually, now that I think about it, back when I was in college, my fraternity brothers used to call me Teddy KGB because I was so good at Hold 'em and my name is—"

"Stay on target, Teddy."

"Oh, right, sorry. Go left here."

Karen waited on the light to change, and followed Teddy's directions.

He continued, "So Irina dragged me into this room, rattled off something in Russian, smiled, and then left me alone with six of the scariest looking dudes ever. I didn't even get a chance to introduce myself before one of them pointed at an empty chair and said in this thick Russian accent, 'Five hundred buy-in.' And I'm like, 'I don't have any money on me,' and he's all, 'No problem. We give good credit. Interest rate is two fingers per week,' and made this motion like he's sawing with a knife. I think I peed myself a little before he started laughing. Take a right here."

"Oh my God, I'm actually kind of impressed."

"Yeah. It wasn't smart."

"What did you do?"

"What could I do? I sat down. The guy said to me, 'I kid, but seriously, five hundred, two fingers per week,' and then started laughing again. Second scariest night of my life, but it's a damn close second to that day in the cabin."

"So you hung out and played poker with the Russian mafia."

"Yep."

"And you made it out alive, apparently."

"They respected me. At least I think they did. You know, mutual poker talent respect. I was up about ten grand before Ivan—he's the fingers guy—said, 'Okay, Smurfboy, you buy answers with that money.'"

Karen giggled. "Smurfboy?"

"Laugh it up, Wallace. I'm used to it."

"Sorry. Then what happened?"

"Nothing much, really. I asked questions, got invited back a couple of times, heard some cool stories, and made a few friends. If I ever get into serious trouble, I know who to call—let's put it that way. Oh, and Ivan wanted me to marry Irina, believe it or not."

Karen pulled up to an intersection. "Which way?" Teddy pointed right and she added with a sarcastic grin, "Marry her? How'd you pass that up?"

Teddy touched her arm—she didn't pull away—

and he said with mock sincerity, "I told him I couldn't, because I was waiting for you."

"Please." Karen laughed and turned into a parking garage. Maybe Teddy was bearable. Not entirely acceptable, but tolerable. "What happened with the game? I don't remember ever hearing about this *Red Mob* thing from Sara."

"Eh, my dad scrapped it when *Juggernaut* really took off, thanks to Sara. Ivan called me at least once a month for two years, asking about it. I haven't heard from him since July. Hopefully he's not pissed at me for never getting his life story into the market."

Karen parked and they got out of the car.

Teddy pointed and said, "It's down this way about two blocks."

"We can get in to speak to him, right? What happens if he's pissed at you?"

"Hell if I know, but I hope it doesn't cost me a few fingers."

ELEVEN

Quirk ran until his chest, lungs, and heart begged for relief.

He paused outside a gluten-free bakery and thought about going inside for a bottle of water. Would it be worth the risk? Most likely his image was all over a series of video surveillance cameras that could trace his path from the parking garage to where he stood now, bent at the waist, heaving and sucking wind. He used to be in such good shape. Back in the Marines he could run miles carrying a fifty-pound rucksack through mountainous terrain and having a conversation as if he were hanging out on a friend's couch.

Now, he wasn't so sure he could sputter the word *help* before collapsing on the ground. He'd come roughly a mile from the parking garage where he'd fired two bullets into Cleo's chest. He could feel the physical—and emotional—weight of her 9mm in his messenger bag.

Quirk glanced around, saw minimal cars and foot traffic, then ducked down a side alley. He took off his windbreaker, his skullcap, and his glasses, then threw them all in a trash bin loaded with the previous day's gluten-free cookies and pastries. Ridding himself of the clothing articles was a minor attempt at disguising his appearance should anyone check the nearby cameras, but the smallest things could help throw the authorities off his trail.

He debated for a moment, and then Cleo's firearm went in, too, after he scrubbed it free of prints as well as he could.

Quirk went into the bakery, grabbed a bottle of water from the cooler, and paid for it. He kept his face pointed away from the woman behind the counter. Ounce of prevention and all that. Was it necessary? Maybe, but maybe not, since it would be a number of days before some sketch artist's rendering of his face was all over the news. He thanked her, she smiled, and he left. Incident-free, but for how long?

Quirk walked slowly until he'd downed the bottle then picked up his pace. He hadn't been thinking clearly as he left the parking garage, and he wondered how much attention he'd drawn to himself by *running* through the streets of downtown Portland not dressed for exercise.

Stupid, he thought. *You know better than that.*

His only solace was that the police wouldn't be on his trail yet. It could be hours before Cleo's body was discovered, hours before the detectives conducted their routine checks, and hours before they reviewed the video feeds and saw him sprinting away. There would be plenty of time to get home, grab some things, and get gone. He only needed a few hours to get an adequate head start.

The exit plan had always been the same. Shave his beard, shave his head, ditch the Portland uniform, and pick up the reserve car, the rusty Camry, and drive. There was a man in northern Washington who had a private plane; they'd take a short trip up to Alaska, and then he'd be on a flight out of Anchorage with his fake identity.

With any luck, the cops, the Feds, whoever, would've shut down the escape routes from the local airports and train stations, but they wouldn't have anticipated his departure from somewhere as far away as Anchorage.

The trick was to go, get on the move, and never look back.

The money he'd earned was untouchable, untraceable, and would be waiting for him once he got to Shanghai. It would work. He knew it would.

By this time next week, he'd be on a small yacht, sipping drinks, relaxing, and hopefully watching some beautiful woman skinny-dip in the sky-blue water.

Quirk wished he'd thought to park his car somewhere away from Powell's. He could use it right now. From his current spot, it was at least three miles back to his home. Walking would take too long. Running would attract attention—no need to make that mistake again.

He raised his hand, waved down a cab, and prayed that the driver was unobservant.

***

The cabbie knew some of the better shortcuts and they made good time. Outside of Quirk's home, there were no police or federal agents waiting for him, which was a great sign.

He ascended his front steps slowly, stepping over the fourth one that always creaked under his weight, and stopping on the porch, he turned and scanned the streets. No unusual cars. No delivery trucks or service vans that could accommodate a couple of FBI guys with a parabolic mic and bottles of stakeout urine tucked in an empty cooler.

So far, so good.

Then the first weird thing happened.

The front door of his house was unlocked. Quirk hesitated before pushing it open. He remembered locking it before he left. Right? He had, hadn't he? Key in, pull the door tighter against the doorjamb to align the latch, and twist. It was the same routine every time.

He frowned. Maybe he had forgotten. He'd been in a hurry and was obsessing over getting to see Cleo again. The traitor. Damn her.

Quirk closed his eyes and inhaled. Time's wasting. There were no other options. He'd gather up some things, make up his mind about the laptop bomb in his basement, and then place the call. *Things got hot, get the plane gassed up*. That call.

He pushed the door open, took two steps inside, and smelled an unfamiliar scent. Perfume, maybe. No—laundry detergent? That after-scent of fabric softener that clings to clean clothes? It wasn't his. He didn't use fabric softener. His skin itched when he did.

Quirk stopped and stood motionless, listening, trying to make his breathing as silent as possible, positive the intruder could hear his heartbeat pounding. The house was old and creaky. The hardwood floors swelled and flexed in the humidity, changing with the temperature fluctuations of Portland's weather. This fact was both a benefit and a disadvantage.

He regretted tossing Cleo's handgun in with the other refuse. The three weapons he owned—a 9mm, a

.45, and a .22 revolver—were all downstairs, along with his fake IDs, his fake passport, and his small stack of get-the-hell-out money.

Downstairs. So far away. Wouldn't it have made more sense to keep them stashed by the door in prep for a hasty exit? Too late now.

Quirk wondered if he was being paranoid, if his senses were all redlining because he'd murdered a fellow…what was she? Fellow murderer? Fellow terrorist? Both? He was on edge, nothing more. That was it. He'd forgotten the door because he'd been thinking about Cleo, and the fabric softener smell could've been coming from the partially open window. Mrs. Lewis, the next-door neighbor, was doing laundry. That made the most sense, didn't it?

He took a deep breath, felt the muscles in his shoulders release, and got halfway to the basement door before a woman pivoted into the living room from where she'd been hiding in the hall.

Gun raised, urging him to stay calm.

Quirk had never seen this woman before, but he knew who she had to be.

The only question remaining was why she was in his house and not directing the mission's objectives from, well, from wherever the hell she called the shots. He imagined Boudica like a Bond villain, hiding in her impenetrable fortress high in the mountains of some tropical island only accessible by helicopter or private jet.

"Easy, Quirk," she said. "Go back and shut that door. We have a lot to talk about." She stepped around his pile of dirty laundry on the floor.

The sound of her voice confirmed it. "Boudica?"

"Over to the couch." She flicked the gun barrel to her left, nudging him. "Hands up where I can see them."

"How long have you been here?"

"Sit. Now."

"Okay." Quirk scooted around the coffee table and lowered himself onto his favorite thrift-store purchase. He'd gotten the couch years ago for twenty bucks, and it had held up well through so many moves. If Boudica shot him, he wondered how the bloodstains would look against the brown material. Probably no different than all the beer, coffee, and chocolate milk stains that blended in with the rest of the pattern.

Boudica said, "I've been here long enough to reconsider killing you."

"Reconsider? Does that mean you'd been *thinking* about it?"

"I'm pretty sure that's how the dictionary defines it, genius."

"No, I mean—why?"

"Doesn't matter. It's a moot point now, anyway. One question for you." She moved in front of the television. "Did you kill Cleo?"

"I—uh—I'm not…"

Boudica took a step closer. "I'm not going to kill you. Not yet anyway, but I know she turned, okay? So what I want to know is if *you* killed her specifically, or if you were with someone else. What I'm asking is did someone else kill her and you escaped, or did you have an accomplice? What happened back there in the garage?"

"Oh God, was that you? When the door opened?"

"Answer the question, Quirk."

"It was me! Okay? Me, I did it. She was working with the FBI and she had me trapped down there, waiting on some guy to show up. She'd turned and I think she was going to get us all arrested or something, or maybe try to get me to be an informant. Something, God, I don't know, but I heard the door to the stairs open and it distracted her just long enough for me to hit her with a chunk of concrete. She went down, I got her gun, *pop-pop,* and she's done. I did you a favor."

"I know you did."

"So does that mean you're still going to kill me?"

"I'm assessing the situation, Quirk."

"That's not...that's not reassuring."

"It wasn't meant to be. You still owe me for London."

"I said I was sorry—"

"*Sorry*?" Boudica laughed. "We're wanted by governments all across the world for international terrorism, Quirk. You don't get to say sorry when you screw up."

"But we did what we wanted to do, didn't we? The guy that owned the game shop, we got him. I thought that's what this whole thing was about. We're proving a point to the world."

"Maybe, but it was too messy, way too messy. Anyway, he wasn't the actual target—"

"He wasn't?"

"Shut up. I'm talking. You, and your brilliant idea to leave the bomb in the actual shop, instead of the second floor of the hotel like I'd asked, almost missed the woman I really wanted. You're lucky she died in the hospital."

"Who was she?" Quirk shook his head. This was the first he'd heard of an alternate mission objective. Bomb the hell out of White's Used Games in London and then wait on the media to discover their information packets in which The Clan claimed responsibility for all the previous attacks, and their written statement regarding the fact that video game violence was a preventable evil.

"Doesn't matter, not to you, anyway. The point is you've stayed loyal, unlike that pixie with a couple of holes in her chest. Nice grouping, by the way."

"Thanks."

"I have Dimitri monitoring the police radio bands. He'll let me know when the bodies have been discovered."

"Who's Dimitri? And did you say *bodies*? Plural?"

"He's the Spirit's…protégé, for lack of a better word and yes, *bodies*. Cleo and the FBI agent handling her."

In more ways than one, Quirk thought. "You got him?"

"He showed up a couple of minutes after you ran up the ramp and disappeared. I'm surprised he didn't see you on his way in."

"I'm sorry."

"Say sorry again and I'll put a bullet between your eyes. What we have to do now is figure out how to finish this screwed-up mess as quickly as we can and then disappear. We're both on video feeds all over downtown Portland and I'd guess that we have less than twenty-four hours before our pictures are on the six o'clock news."

Reluctantly Quirk agreed, feeling the daydreams of blue water and an ocean breeze fading away. At least he wasn't going to die on his couch. Not for a while. "So what do we do?"

"You and I have to find a woman named Sara Winthrop—"

That's the woman that Cleo mentioned.

"—and the Spirit is proceeding with Plan B."

"What's that?"

"Remember the first device you built and gave to Rocket two weeks ago?"

"Yeah."

"*Boom.*"

TWELVE

Sara gnawed on a knuckle, a nervous habit she'd picked up since Shelley's game. The pain reminded her to stay alert and focused. She said, "What was up with Timms back in the office, huh? What made him freak out like that?"

"Somebody messed up his coffee order. Don't change the subject."

"I'm not. I'm wondering if we should be worried about the kids and Miss Willow. Obviously something went wrong."

"I'm sure whatever it was is completely unrelated to your children. The man said it himself, they've got people watching. Don't borrow trouble."

Sara sighed. They were finally moving after at least a thirty-minute delay trying to get across the Burnside Bridge.

Out the window of Barker's car, she watched the world go by. Trees, houses, a pizza joint, a laundry, a convenience store, more houses. Happy little homes where nice families were tucked away inside, cozy and warm, riding out the messy, wet autumn season. Pretty soon the temperature would dip enough to create nasty sheets of ice everywhere. She dreaded the dreary winter.

Maybe the answer was to leave Portland.

Jim had discussed the prospect of opening a satellite office back east. He'd been looking to expand and from the numbers they'd drawn up, moving into a new office and signing a long-term lease made more sense than recruiting and relocation costs.

Brian's remaining family up in Seattle would cause a ruckus about not being able to see the children on a regular basis, but after what he'd put her through, she had every right to make her world her own. The kids would enjoy more opportunities to visit Grandma and Grandpa's farm down in southwest Virginia. The laundry list of benefits was too long to list.

What was holding her in Portland? Nothing.

"Sara?" Barker said.

"Huh?"

"Where'd you go?"

"Virginia."

"Nice there. Got some family in that area."

"I was thinking that once this is over maybe I should take the kids and move back home." She turned to him, watched for his reaction. She had no solid ties to Barker other than a distant friendship and their mutual loss of JonJon, whom Sara didn't even know that well to begin with, but she enjoyed his visits, valued his opinion, and wanted to gauge his response.

The corners of his mouth turned down, not in a frown, but as if he were considering it. He offered a small nod. "Maybe so, but I can't keep an eye on you from three thousand miles away."

"You'd manage to do it somehow." She grinned at him. "Besides, it's just a thought. Jim's been considering an office somewhere back east. We need the talent, but mostly I think it's posturing."

"How so?"

"More offices, we look bigger and more attractive to investors. He's been thinking about going public again."

"Interesting. Does any of *that* have anything to do with this situation? Possibly competitive companies?"

"No. No way. I doubt anybody outside of Jim, Teddy, and I has any clue."

"Good, then stop avoiding the present issue and tell me more about this Boutique, or Bouquet, or Boudica…Crazy Lady, whatever the hell her name is."

"Right, I was hoping you'd forgotten."

"Trust me, young lady, the ol' Bloodhound has still got his wits firing on all cylinders."

Sara watched a maroon Toyota merge in front of them. They eased up to a stoplight.

"I'm waiting."

Sara closed her eyes. "Twenty years ago—was 1993 twenty years ago already? How'd that happen? We were in high school and it was my junior year, and it was the homecoming football game. Every year we played the town just south of us—I mean, God, that rivalry has been going on since my grandparents were in high school. I think we were up by something like four touchdowns at that point, so this group of girls I was trying to hang out with—"

Barker honked his horn. The driver noticed the green light and moved. Barker said, "Wait, *trying* to hang out?"

"It was more like they were evaluating me so they could see if I was cool enough to be a part of their group. Did you ever see *Mean Girls*?"

"No, but I'm divorced from three of them."

Sara laughed. "It's a movie, Barker. You should get out more."

"Did you pass their test?"

Sara's bottom lip quivered. She tried to contain it. "Not after homecoming night. I didn't want anything to do with them."

It had been unseasonably warm that fall, and Sara and the ultra-cool clique of popular girls were strutting around the stadium in their shortest shorts and tank tops, teasing all the high school boys who wanted them but couldn't have them, while the ones the girls wanted were down on the field in sweaty uniforms and tight football pants. Was that what they were called? Football pants? She couldn't remember. Regardless, Troy Thomas was down there, the all-state wide receiver, and through whatever witchcraft the other girls had conjured up, he'd asked her to the dance.

Even back then Sara thought that Julie Harland—the self-appointed leader and master manipulator—had arranged it as a test. Do well with Troy, impress him, maybe offer him an awkward handjob in the back of his Jeep, and she might get accepted as one of the elite. Fail, and it was back to the bottom of the totem pole. There's nothing quite like the pure nastiness behind a teenage girl with a motive.

Sara explained this to Barker, and he nodded knowingly, mumbling something about how none of his ex-wives had grown out of that stage.

Sara said, "It was so warm that night, and like I said, we were already up by so many points that we'd lost interest, and that's not to say we gave a shit about the points anyway, but it was sort of an unwritten rule that we were supposed to keep up with who scored and how, just so we could impress the players later… Anyway, we all walked over to the concession stand on the far side of the field to get popsicles.

"We were standing in line, and like the usual teenage brats, we were gossiping about whoever and whatever, making fun of anybody that wasn't as cool as us. Well, let me rephrase that—they were being jerks, and I was the yes-girl. Don't give me that look, Barker, it's the truth. It made me uncomfortable how…*nasty* they were, and by that time I was already having second thoughts."

"You must've been a rare breed," Barker said.

"Why do you say that?"

"A teenage girl that's waffling over morality versus being popular? I mean, damn, I was never a teenage girl—"

"Are you sure?"

"Don't let my yearbook picture fool you, but what I'm saying is, wouldn't most of them sell their soul to the devil to win the popularity contest?"

"I think some of them do. But yeah, I was having morality issues already."

"See? There's your proof that you're a good soul. You knew the difference back when you were supposed to ignore it for the sake of the wrong kind of attention."

"Not exactly."

"Uh-oh."

"Well, there was Troy to think about. He was so cute and I absolutely didn't want to give up that opportunity, at least not until after the dance, you know? I'd already made up my mind that I was going to go as far as I wanted to with him without going all the way."

"I don't need to hear those details."

"Don't worry—we didn't even go to the dance together, and I heard that he raped a cheerleader in college a couple of years later, so it's a good thing."

"Jesus, yeah. You dodged a bullet. Why didn't you go to the dance?"

"After what happened at the game, I threatened to tell somebody and they told me if I said a word, they'd make my life hell."

"What happened at the game? What'd you do?"

"You mean what *didn't* I do."

Sara recounted how they'd been waiting in line for popsicles and ice cream cones, laughing at some girl for her choice in shoes, when Lucy had spotted Patty Kellog walking behind the opposing team's bleachers. Lucy had pointed and said, "Hey, where do you think Batty Patty is going?"

The four of them had watched as the overweight, frumpy girl ducked out of sight.

Julie had said, "There's nothing back there, let's go

see what she's doing."

And so they had gone. They'd hurried, ignoring the catcalls from horny high school boys and darting past the cute nerds who were too shy to speak. They'd darted past the parents who'd snuck off to the end of the stadium to add a shot of Jim Beam to their fountain sodas, and then, when they'd reached the end of the bleachers, they'd stopped and poked their head around the back side. The opposing team's fans were stomping the metal seats above, cheering and screaming, however hopeless the situation on the field might've been. Sara and the clique couldn't hear a thing aside from the thunderous roar over their heads.

They hadn't been able to see much, either, since the bleachers backed up close to an abandoned factory building about twenty yards away. It blocked the light emanating from Sara's hometown on the other side, and the stadium lights barely penetrated back there.

Barker turned left onto Ellery Road. Sara's house was only a few blocks and a couple of turns away. He said, "Sounds like where we used to go for first base when I was a teenager. Of course, back then we were playing England as the away team."

Sara didn't laugh.

He looked over and saw her wipe at the corner of an eye.

She said, "Julie spotted Patty first and started running toward her, so we all followed like good little lemmings. Poor Patty, she never heard us coming."

"What was she doing? Drinking? Drugs?"

"No—she…you got any tissues in here?" Barker opened the center console and pulled one free of its box. Sara took it, blew her nose, and continued. "She had her shorts down around her ankles and she was squatting on one of the support beams. At first I thought maybe the line for the girl's bathroom was too long, you know? We did it all the time. Sneak off, pee wherever you can. But nope, Patty was…God, I can't even say it out loud. The closer we got, we finally realized she was…she was masturbating."

Surprised, Barker jerked the wheel a little. "*No*. Out in public like that? Why?"

"I have no idea. She wasn't really as off in the head as everyone thought she was—I'd talked to her a few times, like during classes and whatever, and she always seemed a little…misunderstood, I guess. The only thing I can think of is that maybe she was just testing her boundaries for the thrill of it. Does that make sense? Like maybe how people try to have sex in an airplane bathroom."

"So she was more or less joining the Mile High Club by herself underneath the bleachers."

"Right."

"I'm afraid to ask what happened next."

"And I'm embarrassed to tell you."

"You know what, I think I've heard enough. I can get the gist of where it's going, but please tell me you weren't a part of it."

"I've kept this buried for so long, Barker. I never told Brian about it, I've never mentioned it to a therapist…that's how deep it's stayed."

"Now you want to tell *me* to get it off your chest?"

"That's part of it, but maybe it'll help you and Timms understand what's going on inside Patty Kellog's head."

Barker took his eyes off the road and stared at Sara. He could see the shame and pain twisting her features. "I'd rather you tell it to a profiler, but okay. Shoot."

Sara told him about how they'd stopped roughly ten feet from Patty and watched her, and it was then that they had realized what she was doing. Julie had turned to them with a disgusted face and mouthed, "Oh my God." She'd pulled Rebecca, Lucy, Melinda, and Colleen closer, leaving Sara behind, saying to her, "You stand guard."

The four of them had climbed through the bleacher supports, surprised Patty by grabbing her arms, and held her down. She screamed, but no one could hear with the deafening noise overhead, thousands of feet pounding the metal structure above. Julie had flashed a look at Sara—

"It was so *malevolent*," Sara said. "I pretended to laugh because I was honest-to-God scared of her by then. It really hit me how horrible she was. Then the worst part happened, as if it could get any worse. The four of them held that poor girl down and forced her to finish. Lucy was a photographer for the school newspaper and they threatened to take pictures of her and post them all around the school if she didn't."

"Hold on—they forced her to finish masturbating?"

Sara couldn't contain her tears any longer. She whimpered, "Yes."

"Why?"

"Julie kept saying, 'It's your punishment, you dirty whore,' over and over."

"I—uh—wow, I don't even have words for that."

"Who's a good soul now, huh?"

"Come on, you didn't do it. We've all got skeletons we aren't proud of."

"I didn't do it, but I didn't stop it either. Maybe we

all deserve what we get after they did that to her."

Barker turned onto Sara's street and saw her place five houses down. He slowed, creeping along, delaying their arrival so they could finish their conversation. "Listen to me, Sara, you don't deserve shit. I know you. You're a good woman. You're a fantastic mother. Your shell might be a little hard, but you're soft on the inside and I know it. Even if karma exists, and even if it's a bitch, you've already paid, you hear me?"

"Have I? Really? Have I paid enough?"

"The way I see it, yeah."

"I don't know." Sara blew her nose. "Tell me something. Do you think some people are born evil?"

"Possibly."

"Then which is worse, somebody who's born evil, or somebody who becomes evil because they were made that way?"

Barker shook his head. "I've been in this job for a long time, Sara. I've seen the horrible stuff people can do, and I still don't have an answer for that. I don't know if anyone does."

Sara shook her head, her mind refusing to let go of that distant regret. "What if I haven't paid enough, Barker? I didn't stop them and I should've. What if the universe or karma decided that I haven't bled enough for my sins?"

"Sara, stop." Barker parked in front of her house. The lights were on inside. The glow of the television seeped through the thin curtains.

Sara watched the front door, waiting on Jacob or the girls to come running out to greet them.

Barker said, "The past ain't what it used to be. You're a good soul, and you wanna know how I know?"

Sara sniffled. "Yes."

"You're still crying about it twenty years later. If you had evil in your heart, you wouldn't care…you'd be laughing about it, not sitting here regretting what you should've done. End of story, young lady. Now, let's go inside and see your kids. You look at their cute little faces and see those smiles because they're so excited to see you, then you can tell me whether or not you've paid enough, okay?"

Sara nodded.

Barker squeezed her hand.

They got out and started across the street.

The force of the deafening explosion lifted them into the air and threw them back against the side of the car.

THIRTEEN

Teddy led Karen into Firebrand not knowing what to expect. He hadn't been there in months, but from what he could see it didn't matter, because the place hadn't changed. It had a rather unique western theme in that there were murals of cowboys on the walls, dressed in their rustic open-range gear. Wide-brimmed hats, boots with spurs, and long dusters that stretched down to their ankles. It could be seen as normal if all the cowboys weren't cartoonish aliens with green skin, wide, round eyes, and snaggletooth smiles.

Alien cowboys herding alien-looking cattle, having gunfights with Native Americans, or sitting around campfires.

Teddy had often thought about asking Ivan, the owner, where in the hell he'd gotten his inspiration, but knowing Ivan, it was nothing more than his odd, eclectic Russian taste. A touch of the weird, just because.

There were cactus plants and the swinging double doors of a saloon. Pistols and holsters hung behind the bar. Teddy remembered that the last time he'd been there, they'd served him a sarsaparilla float. As if every night wasn't western-themed, Thursday nights were specifically designated Western Night, and the ladies got free drinks if they came to the bar dressed as cowgirls. Which, of course, meant it was Teddy's favorite night to visit Ivan and hear more stories of his time with the Red Mob.

Now, on Saturday at around noon, the place was close to empty except for the lone man at the bar eating peanuts and watching soccer on the flat-screen that hung above the rows and rows of liquor bottles.

Teddy pointed to the man and told Karen, "That's Ivan's brother, Oleg. He wrestled for Mother Russia in the Olympics. They called him The Bear."

Impressed, Karen nodded and said, "He looks like he could eat one for breakfast."

"Don't be surprised if he spits out a claw. That dude scares the crap out of me."

Oleg turned, saw Teddy, and gave a quick flick of his chin to say hello.

Teddy whispered, "He doesn't like me that much."

"Why?"

"You've met me, right? Do most people need a reason?"

"You're not so bad."

"Right."

A young blonde woman emerged from a doorway

to the right of the bar. She was tall and thin with a sparkling smile and bright blue eyes that could be seen across the room. She wiped her hands on a rag, asked Oleg if he wanted another round, and then spotted Teddy and Karen standing near the doorway. "Howdy, stranger!"

To Teddy, hearing a western twang coupled with a Russian accent was impossibly cute. "Hey, Irina."

He hadn't seen her in months. She looked fantastic. She had a brighter glow to her skin and she'd put on a couple of healthy, much-needed pounds. He imagined that if she were to lift her shirt, he wouldn't be able to play her ribs like a xylophone. The last time he'd talked to her, she was close to getting her braces removed—he waited on her to smile again—yes, perfection. White and straight, giving her a look that suggested professional tennis star instead of meth addict.

Maybe Ivan had the right idea. Now that she'd straightened herself out, worked a proper job, got off whatever drugs she'd been addicted to back when they first met, he could see the possibilities. But then, there was the woman standing next to him—

Karen cleared her throat.

Teddy blinked and refocused on the present. "Right, Karen, this is Irina, she's Ivan's granddaughter."

"Hi, Irina."

"Howdy."

Teddy smirked as they moved over to the bar. "What's with the accent?"

"It's a new thing, y'all. Grandpa says it gives the place more flavor, so I gotta talk like a sweet lil' cowgirl while I'm working."

Oleg grunted. "Is bullshit. Disgrace to our homeland."

Irina giggled and threw the wet bar towel at him. "The Bear is grouchy this morning. Y'all want a drink?"

"No, thank you," Karen said. "We're sort of in a rush."

"You sure? On the house."

Teddy said, "We can't. We're actually looking for someone and wanted to know if we could speak to Ivan for a couple of minutes."

"Sure thing, sweetheart, y'all come on back. I hope you remember how to play cards."

"Oh, I haven't forgotten."

Karen flashed a look at Teddy. "We don't have time for that."

"We may not have a choice."

As they left the main bar, where the air smelled like stale beer and cleaning solution with subtle undertones of western leather, they crossed into the backroom and stepped into a murky haze where the cigar smoke hung nearly impenetrable over the heads of six men sitting around a table.

Irina, dropping the accent but speaking in English as a courtesy to Teddy and Karen, said, "Grandpa, look who's here—your favorite son."

Karen leaned over and whispered in Teddy's ear, "Favorite son?"

"Son-in-law." Teddy took a closer look at Ivan once they'd reached the perimeter of the table. The fluorescent bulb overhead broke through the thick fog of cigar smoke. Ivan didn't look so well. His hair was uncombed. He'd lost weight. His skin looked sallow and saggy around his cheeks and eyes. The oxygen tubes, extending from the tank to his left, hung across his ears, but the tips lay limply at his chest instead of in his nose where they belonged.

Teddy's heart ached. He'd never gotten over his healthy fear of the old man, but the relic drooping in his chair was not the terrifying brute he'd once been. And so quickly. Six months? If that?

Irina scolded Ivan for not having the oxygen tubes

inserted into his nostrils. She fussed around him, fixed his hair, and helped him guide them in. "All this smoke in here, Grandpa, you shouldn't do this anymore."

Pride has a way of trumping sickness.

A year ago Ivan would've chased Irina out of the room, swatting her with a rolled up newspaper for speaking to him like that in front of his friends and partners. Instead, he smiled warmly at her, patted her cheek, and asked for another cup of green tea. Irina said to Teddy, "Keep an eye on him," and then left them alone.

"Ivan," Teddy said, "you look like hell. Did one of these jokers beat you up?" He patted Andrei on the shoulder, the man who used to be Ivan's former bodyguard back during the Cold War. Andrei took his hand, squeezed, and shook.

Ivan croaked, "My boy. Come see me," and waved Teddy over.

Teddy eased around the table, shook Ivan's hand, and then allowed the old man to pull him down for a hug.

"Who's your friend?"

"This is Karen Wallace. She's—" Teddy hesitated, unsure of how the group would react to a former FBI agent and current private investigator amongst them. "She's a friend of mine."

Karen smiled, waved, said hello, and kept her distance.

Ivan winked at Karen. "Not a girlfriend, I hope. You know, Teddy, my Irina is still single."

"She looks amazing."

"Thank you. All for you. Let me know when you're ready. Anyway, anyway, where are my manners—we need to introduce your friend. Karen Wallace, say hello to Andrei, Viktor, Boris, Yefim, and Nikolai. The best Mother Russia had to offer, and now the worst Uncle Sam has seen."

Karen stepped forward, waved, and responded with smiles as a chorus of greetings filled the room in broken English.

Ivan said, "You have time for a game? We could use some fresh meat in the pot. Three fingers over prime rate, as always." He laughed, and so did his comrades.

Boris, the white-haired, decrepit flower-shop owner and former hitman, said, "Ivan, please. He takes all our cash. I'm short on rent this month. Go away, Smurfboy. You're not welcome." He laughed too, as did the others.

Teddy put his hands in his pockets. "Unfortunately, as much as I'd love to steal your lunch money, Boris, we don't have time."

Irina returned, carrying a steaming mug of green tea. The string was twisted around the handle. Teddy recalled teaching her that trick. She smiled at him as she set the tea in front of Ivan.

Teddy felt a warm pull in his stomach when she bent over. What was that? Longing? He returned her smile and made up his mind to come back and visit her soon.

Should he? Why not?

Karen was out of his league and he knew it. And Irina was too, for that matter, but at least she didn't grimace whenever he walked into a room. He'd been working with his therapist on reading and processing social cues. Sara had mentioned recently that he'd shown some progress around the office, but he couldn't tell if she was telling the truth or falsely encouraging him.

"Actually," he said, "we're here to ask you for a small favor, Ivan."

"For my favorite son, anything. What do you need? Come, sit. Sit. Andrei, make some room for my boy." Andrei scooted to the side and pulled another chair around for Teddy to sit. "Join us, Karen Wallace. We're not such rude old men like we seem—we'll make room."

"No, thank you. I'll stand."

Ivan nodded. "You're young, one day you'll sit." He returned his attention to Teddy. "Tell Ivan what he can do for you, Smurfboy."

"We're looking for someone." Teddy watched as Karen stepped closer, arms crossed, waiting to get involved, if necessary. Or perhaps she was ready to shut him up if he said too much. He'd been working on that, too. "It's sort of a long shot and I don't know if you would even have the slightest clue who this guy might be…he's a Russian here in the States now, and we think he has some business here in Portland."

"And you think just because we're Russian, we know this man?"

"I…uh…well, the thing is, Ivan, he's sort of…we think he does *underground* work, if you know what I mean." Teddy swallowed hard. He hoped that he'd managed to convey his point without offending anyone. Ivan would be fine, he was sure of it, but Viktor and Nikolai could be temperamental.

Ivan raised his chin. "Mmm-hmm." He reached down to his side and twisted the valve of the oxygen tank, turning it off.

Karen added, "I think what Teddy means is—"

Ivan held up a hand. "I know what he means," he said, then faced Karen. "My apologies for interrupting. I get annoyed when I learn of comrades doing *underground* work, as Teddy says, without coming to see me first."

"He's extremely dangerous."

"And we're not?"

Teddy sensed the need to step in before Karen dug her hole any deeper. Former FBI, private investigator, whatever authoritative, mental mode she was currently in wouldn't hold up against the bravado of the retired Russian mafia. Teddy wanted to say, "Finesse, Karen. Be a ballerina, not a bulldozer." He'd heard Detective Barker say that a while back. Barker wouldn't mind if he used it.

Instead, he told Ivan, "A friend of ours is in trouble. Do you remember me telling you about Sara, the woman that works with me?"

"I do. She had the kidnapping game with her kids."

"Right, her."

"She's doing well?"

"No, not actually. She's—"

"Again with this woman? What now?"

"I wish we could tell you, but I think the official phrase is…Karen, help me out here."

"We're not at liberty to say."

"Yeah, that."

Boris laughed. "Fuck your liberty."

"Boris!" Ivan snapped. "Respect the guests, please."

Boris hung his head and offered a small, apologetic wave. "Joking, joking."

"Who is this man, Teddy? Tell me his name."

"Karen will have to confirm it for sure, but as far as I know, it's Vadim Bariskov," Teddy said, tensing when the men around him flinched. They knew the name, it seemed, and weren't too excited by the fact. "He also goes by—"

Ivan pounded the table with his fist. Poker chips bounced and drink glasses rattled. Andrei's soda toppled over. Ivan said, "The Spirit. Andrei, did you know this man was in town?"

Andrei stuttered, "N-n-no."

"Did anyone?"

The other four men muttered a combination of responses in Russian and mixed English, all amounting to, "We had no idea."

Teddy said, "So I guess you know him."

Ivan took a sip of his green tea and nodded. "Yes. Ex-KGB. Caused me years of trouble. I would rip out his heart and feed it to Andrei if we ever crossed paths again."

"Then maybe we can do something about that. We're kind of in a rush, and it's important so we can help Sara. Would you have any idea how we can find him?"

Ivan drummed his fingers on the table.

Teddy couldn't tell if it was anger, fear, or something else in the old Russian's eyes.

Ivan said, "You don't find the Spirit. The Spirit finds you."

FOURTEEN

Quirk drove the dark blue Honda while Boudica called the remainder of the group. Most of them were stationed around Portland in various locations, waiting to execute additional stages of her plans. She'd mentioned that Plan B was in effect because Cleo's betrayal to the FBI had left her with no choice. Quirk had no idea what Plan A had been, much less what the details of Plan B were. His only task had been to build the bombs and deliver them to Rocket when necessary, and when asked.

Boudica's first phone call was to Chief, whom Quirk had met once to finalize a minor detail, without her knowledge. She said, "How in the hell did you miss it, Chief? Cleo was the—Jesus, it sounds so stupid when I say it out loud, but she was the double agent, playing both sides. Listen to me, do not let it happen again, or I will personally fly to D.C. and I will slit your throat while you sit there in your little cubicle. I don't care if it's the FBI headquarters or not, do you hear me? If you miss something like that again, I'm going to march straight down Pennsylvania Avenue, through those front doors, and I will find you. Don't apologize;

it's too late. Find out what Timms did with Sara Winthrop and call me back as soon as you know something. Then, if you've managed to do that without screwing up, get me everything you can on Melinda Wilkes in Paris. Do you need to ask when? I wanted it yesterday."

Her second phone call was to Sharkfin. Quirk had never met her before, but from some of the minor details he'd gathered from Cleo she was the "gatherer" of the group, for lack of a better term. Passports, IDs, flight information, and FBI movements were only some of the things she was responsible for. Sharkfin had been the one to find the exotic explosive material after DarkTrade's demise. Boudica said to her, "We've moved on to Plan B. I don't have time to explain everything, but let's just say that your shares are only getting split five ways now. We need a brand new set of everything for all of us. IDs, driver's licenses—U.S. and French both—new tickets to Paris. Everything. We're new people. Yes, that's right…all except for Cleo."

The sound of her name sent an uncomfortable tremor through Quirk's stomach.

He regretted what had happened to her, what he'd done to her—he couldn't make an obsession that had held strong for nearly two years disappear in an afternoon, not completely… Yet she'd betrayed them. She was going to turn him in to the FBI.

Boudica brought up an excellent point. Their pay would only be split five ways.

Quirk signaled, drove up the entrance ramp to the interstate. *Five ways*, he thought. *More for me, less for turncoats.*

Third, she called Rocket. "How'd it go? Are you there now? Jesus, don't get too close, idiot. What if they spot you? I'm sure it's beautiful, psycho, but if you get caught standing around admiring your work, you just remember what happens if they're able to get information out of you. Oh, it'll be worse than that. Listen, do me a favor and get out of there before it comes to that, okay? All right, I'll check in later. Whoa, what? She's there now? She saw it happen? Don't you think that's the first thing you should've told me? What's she's doing right now? You're kidding. Sometimes the universe aligns, huh? Damn it, I can't believe I'm missing that. Rocket? Hey, stay back. I said stay back. Keep your distance. I'll call Tank and let him take care of it. I said forget it. Don't let Sara Winthrop out of your sight, and if she's escorted away before Tank gets there, pay attention to which vehicle. He'll be in touch."

Boudica slapped the burner shut and shook her

head. "Did *you* tell me to hire Rocket?"

"No." Quirk checked the mirrors. "He was…I think Cleo knew him. His brother was the one who died—"

"I don't care. But Cleo, that explains it. Anyway, it sounds like Plan B is going well so far, despite the fact that Rocket is in the crowd, staring at her house from across the street. Moron. The good news is, I think—well, I hope—he's too stupid to reveal much of anything important."

"Right. What *is* Plan B, exactly?" Quirk drove, not knowing where to go. At the moment, all he needed to do was keep the Honda between the lines. He risked a look at Boudica, paranoid that eye contact with her might turn him to stone like Medusa.

Now that he'd gotten a little closer to the woman in charge and had gotten a peek behind the curtain, he wasn't so sure what the main plan had been after all. The irony wasn't lost on him; blowing up buildings, and people, to prove the point that video games caused violence and that it was a preventable issue, but the more he listened to Boudica, the more he thought there were hidden motives behind her methods.

Boudica tapped the cheap cell phone against her knee, staring at him. She brushed a strand of wavy brunette hair out of her face and tucked it behind an ear. "You do realize I should kill you just for asking, don't you? Or have you totally forgotten that the left hand isn't supposed to know what the right hand is doing?"

"No, I was curious, that's all. I mean, it'd be nice to know if one of my creations did what it was supposed to do. Like your kid getting a word right in the spelling bee. Just…never mind. I won't ask again. Lips are sealed, you can forget I even brought it up."

"Quirk?"

"Huh?"

"Shut up."

"Yes, ma'am."

"Keep driving while I call Tank, then maybe we'll talk. Can you do that much?"

"Yes, ma'am."

Boudica dialed yet another number, and Quirk once again listened to her side of the conversation. "Tank, change of plans. I know you're as clueless as the dingleberry sitting here beside me, but we've got Plan B in effect. There's always been a Plan B. Yes. If you think you can—quiet, or I'll have to give the Spirit a call."

Boudica covered the mouthpiece with her hand and said to Quirk, "What's with you people? I feel like a goddamn kindergarten teacher trying to keep you whiny brats under control."

Then, to Tank, she added, "Yes, Tank, I *understand* it's not good when plans change, but since we don't live inside a TV show, circumstances adjust themselves accordingly. So here's what I need you to do: get over to what's left of Sara Winthrop's house and monitor the situation from a distance. Don't let Rocket see you or he'll probably wet his pants like an overexcited Chihuahua. Yeah, he's there—only engage if you can't locate Sara Winthrop. If Rocket can keep himself out of handcuffs, he'll be keeping an eye on her. If she's still there when you arrive, hang tight, and once she's escorted away, give it some distance, and then you intercept. Got it? They'll probably need the manpower there to take care of the bodies inside or to scan the area, so more than likely she'll be in an ambulance with minimal supervision, if any at all. Call me once you have her secure."

Boudica hung up, rolled down the window, and paused before tossing the disposable out onto the highway. "I should probably keep this. I don't have any spares until we meet up with Sharkfin again."

"Is that where we're going?"

"No. We're killing time until Tank can get that bitch to the drop point. Then, if I haven't killed you yet, maybe we can have a little fun together, huh?"

"If that's what you want, yeah." Quirk realized those options were likely the best he was going to get. Dying, or having fun watching…whatever it was that Boudica planned to do to this woman.

She reached over and ran the back of her knuckles down his cheek, caressing his jawline, then tugging his beard gently, playfully.

Quirk realized he'd misunderstood her definition of "fun." What in the hell was she doing?

"You've earned yourself a few more days, I guess. There's Paris to take care of, and then…who knows? Besides," Boudica said, sliding her fingers over to his ear, softly stroking the lobe. "We have some time to kill."

Quirk flinched. "Uh, wh-what do you—"

"Relax," she said, leaning over to him, putting her hand on his thigh. She eased it up toward his crotch, digging in with her fingernails at the same time. "Doesn't all of this turn you on? So close to being caught, always right on the edge of destruction. Tell me…*Mark*…what's your fantasy?"

He could feel her warm breath on his neck. Her hand slid closer to the flaccid lump in his pants. Boudica was attractive—much more attractive than he'd expected, and under normal circumstances, these advances would be welcome. But, she was also terrifying in a demented, sadistic, lady-terrorist sort of way, which helped keep the unwanted erection under control.

"Oh, uh, fantasies, fantasies—I don't really have any. So you, um, you like being caught? That's yours?" He fidgeted and tried to turn away from her teeth on his earlobe. He eased up on the gas pedal. Eighty-five miles per hour wasn't the safest or the most intelligent speed.

Boudica cupped his crotch and squeezed, traced her fingers up, and then tugged at his zipper. "So close to being caught," she said. "The chance is always *right there.*" She slid a hand underneath his shirt and pinched a nipple.

Quirk winced.

She asked, "Have you ever been caught?"

"Caught doing what?"

"Come on," she purred, "don't make me say it."

Quirk cringed. He was rarely lost. He'd always been a quick thinker, a particularly useful skill that had gotten him out of many groundings in high school, had saved his ass from a drill instructor's wrath more times than he could count, and had saved his life at least three times in Iraq. This situation with Boudica, however, was an entirely different monster altogether, and he was utterly clueless about how to proceed. Give in and entertain her lustful insanity or reject her and risk…what? A bullet to the head?

Some unfortunate hiker or hunter would discover his body in a few days, sitting lifeless and decomposing in the driver's seat of a blue Honda.

On the other hand, if he could make it out of this alive, he had a lot to look forward to, especially the twenty-footer he'd be sailing on in three months at the most.

Boudica was insane, yeah, but who was he to judge? The bombs he'd made for her had killed a dozen people around the world already, with many more on the horizon, and from the sound of it, there'd been more within the past hour.

He tried to convince himself that he could endure long enough to survive.

I'm crazy, he thought. *She's crazy. She's goddamn scary but still, she's hot, right? In that demented dominatrix way, at least? I could do it. I could do this. There's gotta be worse things than sex to stay alive. Stop it. Stop trying to talk yourself into this. Think of something.*

Boudica suckled his earlobe and pulled at it with her teeth. "I told you not to make me say it. Have you been caught before? I got caught once. Do you want me to tell you about—" The disposable phone buzzed in her lap.

She shoved herself away from him, frustrated, and snapped the phone open. "What?"

Quirk loosened his grip on the steering wheel. His fingers ached.

"Are you sure?" she asked. "Okay, good work, Rocket. Let Tank know. Yes, you're done. See you in Paris. It's in France. I'm sure you can get French fries. Goodbye, Rocket." She slammed the phone closed, threw it in the floorboard, and punched the glove compartment. Three deep breaths later, she said, "If he wasn't so good at what he does, I'd kill him myself, just to keep him from contaminating the gene pool. God help us if that guy ever breeds."

Quirk forced a laugh. He expected her to say, "Where were we?"

Instead, she gave him instructions to Coffee Creek Correctional Facility. Simple, calm, and authoritative, as if her hand hadn't been down his pants thirty seconds ago.

Yeah. Crazy.

"Why there?" he asked.

"We're going to see someone who didn't finish her job. By that time, Tank should have Sara Winthrop where we want her."

FIFTEEN

Sara opened her eyes. She was confused, groggy, and the muffled hum in her ears drowned out everything except the high-pitched ringing. Her head hurt, as did her back and sides. She was on the ground. Why was she on the ground?

There was a muffled pounding in her head. Was that her heartbeat? Next came the dulled voice of someone beside her. Words shouted through thick walls. Who was that?

What happened?

A piece of flaming wood fell at her side. She studied it, uncomprehending.

Fire. That's fire. Move away. Move.

Wait, that's Barker's car. Fire in the middle of the street. Wood on fire.

The voice came again. "Sara? Sara, are you okay?" Clearer than before, but masked as if filtered through a pillow.

Hands on her back, her shoulders, twisting her tenderly. "You're bleeding. Can you hear me?"

She turned her head. Pain arced through her neck and her vision muddled. When it cleared, she could see

Barker kneeling at her side. A trickle of blood ran down his forehead. A piece of ash landed on his mustache as he touched her cheek and checked her eyes. He repeated, "Can you hear me?"

Sara nodded and tried to get up.

Barker urged her to stay down.

"I—I need to…what? Barker?"

Screaming. She could hear screaming in the distance. The thick shroud over her hearing slowly dissipated as she tried to regain her bearings. More flaming wood behind Barker. Shards of glass glinting on the blacktop like stars in the street.

Motion. Movement. People running, shouting for help.

Barker said, "It's going to be okay. We've got help coming. I'm sure…I'm sure there's some hope."

Hope? Why hope? What did Barker mean by that? Dizzy, Sara sat upright and glanced around her. Glass in the street. Flaming wood. A singed teddy bear, ripped, with stuffing protruding from a spot where a leg had been. A purple teddy bear with a white heart on its chest. *That's—is that—?*

"Lacey!" Sara tried to stand again and Barker grabbed her arm.

"Sara, don't. You're hurt. We need to—"

She tried to sling his arm away. "My kids. Where

are—get off me. Barker, let go. Let go of me now!" She wrenched free of his grasp and stumbled when she tried to stand. She fell against his car and paused, allowing her vision to clear, feeling something warm creep down the bridge of her nose and into her right eye. Blood. She wiped it away and inhaled, centering herself.

Once the dizziness passed, she saw the unfathomable destruction.

Her home was a smoldering pile of rubble. Gone. All of it. Disintegrated into a mass of burning siding, shredded shingles, and splintered, smoking wood. There were pieces of her history laying everywhere. In the yard, in the street, on top of cars. Where once had been a life, however broken it may have seemed at times, now resided an empty spot. A hole in her heart. There, and then not there.

Were those sirens?

She screamed, "No!" and tried to run toward it. Barker grabbed her, held her back. She kicked, fought, and tried to break free. Screaming the names of her children. They'd been inside. The three of them with Miss Willow, waiting on her to get home. She should've been in there. She should've been with them. She should've disappeared into a red mist along with them. Her life, her family. Everything she had to live for.

Gone.

The unbearable agony sent her to the ground, emotions exploding within. Detonations of anger, loss, and regret tore her insides apart, pulling so hard that she was unable to cry. Her mouth hung open, lips pulling down at the corners, stretching into an image of wretched misery.

Why? Why, God, why?

Barker sat beside her, wrapped his arms around her shoulders and pulled close. It was all he had to offer.

Sara's shoulders heaved as the sobs finally broke free. She clenched Barker's shirt and pulled, burying her face into his chest. She let go. She let the flood of tears come.

Barker stroked her hair. He waited.

The sirens approached. Fire, medical, police.

"It's not your fault," he said, gently rocking her. "There's no—"

Sara let go and slammed her fist into his chest, not from anger, but misery.

"I'm sorry, Sara."

"They're gone."

"Don't say that. Not yet." He looked at the fiery

remains of the home. Maybe they were—there was always the possibility—

Sara pulled away from him and rolled onto her side. She shoved the nearest piece of flaming wood to the side. She could taste blood on her tongue, that metallic taste of a wound—emotional and physical alike. The ragged, rough edges of the blacktop dug into her cheek. She held her sides and curled into a ball, listening to the wailing sirens, the screaming, the sounds of her broken, shattered home settling…the sounds of her life ending.

Barker stood. “There’s the ambulance. Can you walk? Never mind, stay there. You might have a concussion. Hey, over here! Hurry! Over here, now, damn you!” Approaching footsteps followed. “She’s got a serious laceration to the head. Maybe a concussion. Over here, yeah. Sara? Do you have any nausea?”

Sara looked up to see the young paramedic leaning over her, who said, “Ma’am, can you see me okay? Hearing?” Sara told him she wanted to be left alone. “I’m sure you do, but I need to check on you anyway, okay? Follow this light for me.”

Sara followed his penlight with her eyes.

“Looks like you hit your head pretty hard, but your speech is okay. No nausea? Confusion?”

"I'm fine," she said again. Physically, yes, but mentally…life would never be the same.

She heard Barker say, "That wound on her head is deep. She'll probably need stitches."

"Looks like it, yeah. Hold this here, if you don't mind."

Sara felt pressure on the side of her head. Something soft. Gauze, maybe. Barker's hand held it there. She should've been in pain. She could feel nothing but an overwhelming numbness. She stared straight ahead while the paramedic tried to treat her remaining injuries as she lay on her side.

In front of her and underneath Tom Jessup's car, the neighbor to her right, she noticed one of Jacob's shoes—the ones with lights in the soles that he'd begged and pleaded for over the summer. The explosion had damaged whatever machinations were inside the soft rubber, and she watched as the lights blinked from red, to blue, to green, to orange, and back to red. The cycle repeated like runway lights guiding an airplane in, safely delivering its passengers.

She felt the despair, the loss, somewhere deep inside, but the numbness and disbelief jammed it back down.

She heard Barker tell the paramedic, "We need to keep an eye on her, okay? That was *her* house.

Her…her…" Sara could sense that Barker was having trouble with the reality, too.

She finished the sentence for him. "My family was in there."

The paramedic said, "Is anyone in the house?"

Barker stopped him. "Jesus, Mary, and Joseph. Sara. Sara, get up. Can you get up?" She turned an eye up to Barker standing overhead, but nothing more. She made no effort. He stared at something, a small smile arcing upward at the corners of his lips. "Help me get her to her feet."

Numb. Dazed. Lost. Hands hooked under her armpits. There was a sense of lifting while gravity and pain tried their best to pull her back down.

Barker said, "Look, Sara," and pointed toward the back of the gathering crowd.

"What?" she mumbled. "What am I—Willow!"

Miss Willow looked up. Her eyes went wide. Fear dissolved into relief on her face. She began shoving her way through the crowd, saying, "Excuse me! Can we get through? We need to see that woman, please."

We. That one simple word sent Sara's world into heartening mixture of gratitude and staggering joy. She stumbled around the front of Barker's car, lurching toward them as he grabbed an arm, helping her regain her balance.

Miss Willow broke through the crowd of onlookers. Jacob was in front of her. Lacey and Callie followed at her sides, each holding a hand.

Lacey and Callie shouted in unison, "Mama!"

Jacob was next with a relieved, "Mommy!"

Sara fell to her knees. She pulled all three of them in close, hugging them as if she would never let go.

She heard Barker say, "It don't happen often, but once in a while there's a goddamn miracle when you need it."

"Oh my God," Sara said, "I thought you were…Mommy thought—" She couldn't say the words. Not out loud. Saying the words out loud might make it real, it might take them away. "Where *were* you guys?"

"At the park," Jacob answered.

Sara looked up at Miss Willow, whose words came out in a nervous, shaky, rambling rush. "I have to tell you something, and it's going to sound crazy, but about fifteen minutes ago, someone called the house. I didn't recognize the number on the caller ID, but I answered it anyway because sometimes you get calls from those gaming magazine reporters and I figured it was easier to tell them not right now than to leave you to deal with it and, and—"

"Willow, what're you talking about?"

"Someone, I don't know who—he sounded older and like maybe he was…I can't even tell you what, it was so weird—but he said…he told us that we needed to leave the house, that you'd requested somebody from the police department to come by and run a sweep for bugs and it would be better if we were out of the way. He said you told him."

"And he didn't say who he was?"

Barker said, "Whoa, somebody warned you?"

Miss Willow nodded. "I almost didn't listen to him. It sounded so peculiar but maybe it was intuition or God or who knows, but he said we needed to leave the house, that it was a…I think he said 'necessary precaution,' and he said you'd requested him to call."

"And he didn't identify himself?" Barker asked, trying to confirm.

Sara added, "Think, Willow, did he?"

"No, not that I remember. Sara, who would… I'm sorry, I'm so sorry."

Barker said, "Stay right here. I'll get somebody working on the phone records right now. Be back in a sec. Donaldson? Hey, Donaldson!" Barker moved away, walking toward a uniformed officer talking on his CB.

Sara chewed on the inside of her bottom lip. Who would call and tip off her family before blowing up her home? Was it a warning? Maybe it was a shot fired across the bow, telling her, "Look what we can do."

She shook her head. It mattered, but not right now. Her family was alive, safe, and standing in front of her.

Sara stood. She pulled Miss Willow and the children into a hug. "It's okay. Barker will figure it out. The only thing that matters is that you guys weren't in there. I thought I lost you all." She hugged Willow tighter then bent over and kissed the twins, then Jacob on top of the head. She glanced over at Barker and saw him smiling. The paramedic started to say something as he pointed at her head, but Barker shooed him away.

Some of the bystanders nearby had overheard and observed their little reunion and converged, asking if that was Sara's house and what happened and thank the Good Lord above that no one had been inside. Sara smiled and nodded, saying thank you but overwhelmed by the attention. She moved back a step and pulled her group along as well.

Barker returned and moved in front of them, urging the crowd to give them room, telling the throng of onlookers that they were now contaminating a crime scene and needed to back away, they needed to watch their step, and not to trample anything that might look like evidence. He called over some uniformed policemen and urged them into crowd control. "Rope if off, too," he said. "I want everything within the damage zone cordoned off, got it?"

"Yes, sir," one of the policemen said.

Barker marched toward Sara, all business now, transitioning into detective mode. "We'll get a look at the phone records as soon as possible."

"Good."

"Meanwhile we need to get you guys out of here, but not until they've finished checking you out. That paramedic needs to fix you up, then we'll go."

"We need to get out of here, right now."

"We will, I promise, but you're hurt and I need to brief some of the others. I need a few minutes, that's all. Besides, this is probably the safest place for you at the moment. Look at all this firepower."

"Kids, stay next to me, please," Sara said, motioning for her children to come closer. "Maybe you're right. Goddamn it. That was our *home*, Barker. And look at the neighbors' homes. Somebody needs to tell them, too. Seriously, I have to apologize whenever they get here. Their places are ruined because of me."

"Not because of you. Blame it on whoever built that bomb, you hear me? There'll be plenty of time later for apologies but at the moment, you need fixing, and then you need to be gone."

Barker marched toward an ambulance with open doors. Sara followed with her family close behind, saying, "I changed my mind, Barker. I think we should go."

"Trust me, we're safer here for the time being. Just keep the kids away from the wreckage."

"Sara," Miss Willow said, "who would do such a thing? What's going on? Did that Sergeant girl get out of prison?"

Sara shook her head. "I'll explain later."

Lacey said, "Look! My bear," and moved toward the smoldering, ragged mess of stuffing and purple material on the street.

"Leave it." Sara pulled at her arm.

"But she's mine."

"Mr. Bloodhound needs it for evidence, okay? You have to leave it there. We'll get you another one."

Jacob asked, "Is our stuff still in there, Mom?"

Mom? Not Mommy, Sara thought. *When did that start?*

"Not anymore, honey. Nothing that's worth saving."

Barker touched her shoulder. "Sara."

"Yeah?"

"Let him do his job."

The paramedic looked closely at her wound.

Sara glanced around. They were at the ambulance already. How hard had she hit her head?

Barker added, "We'll get you guys out of here soon, okay? Somewhere safe."

"Where is safe? If they can get to my home, what's to say they can't find me anywhere else, huh?"

"I'll have some of the men take you down to the station. Full escort. You'll be fine."

"That's what you said on the way over here."

"I…I know. We couldn't have seen this coming."

"What if they ambush us on the way to the station? Then where do we go? Or, supposing we make it, how long are we supposed to stay? Maybe you can have the chief bring in a decorator and cozy up one of the cells for us."

Barker reached for a cigarette and grumbled when he found a container of cinnamon toothpicks. He pulled one free and stuck it in his mouth, chewing on it, grinding it between his teeth. "I understand it's not the best option—"

"Jim's house," Sara said. "Remember? He mentioned the panic room."

"That's probably designed for short-term use, Sara. We'll do everything we can to find this group of assholes—sorry, kids—this group of *jerks* and keep y'all safe, but I can't promise it'll happen today, or even tomorrow. I need to find Timms and brief him, then we need to start pulling things together here. We'll get going as soon as possible."

The paramedic tried to get her to lie down. She shoved him away.

"Stop for a second, please?" she said, then to Barker, "We're not going anywhere without you. I don't care what has to happen, just get us to Jim's house and put us in a big metal bunker until this is over with. I don't trust anyone else except for you and him. Teddy, too, I guess, but who knows what he's doing with Karen."

"Okay, if that's the way you want it. I'll have a convoy escort you to Jim's—"

"*No*, you're coming too. Not without you. Not an option."

"Sara, I can't leave. We need to get started on the investigation."

"Take us and come back, or we'll hide in the back of one of those cruisers until you're ready to go."

Barker considered it for a moment. He pulled the toothpick from his mouth and flicked it on the ground. He paused a moment, thinking, watching the commotion of officers, firefighters, and medics working their hardest. "Okay, but here's the deal: You let Skippy here fix you up, and get these kids and

Willow in the back of that ambulance and out of sight."

"Thank you."

"Hold on now. I'm not done yet. When he's finished, I want all five of you to get in my car and wait. Stay low, lock the doors, and don't speak to anyone. Let me talk to a couple of guys here and I'll be right back."

"How long?"

"I don't know, but I can't just walk away. Not yet. Not after this."

***

Thirty minutes later, Sara, Miss Willow, and the children climbed into Barker's car and waited. At least she thought it had been thirty minutes. Whether it was the emotional shock of thinking her family had died or the blow to her head, things seemed off. Time and distance were fuzzy.

Sara pushed a button on his radio. The LED display told her an hour had passed. She wondered if she should have the paramedic check her for a concussion again. It was easy to get lost in the chaos.

As they sat waiting on Barker, Sara noticed two men on the edge of the crowd. They appeared to be quietly arguing, and then both of them turned to stare at her in unison.

SIXTEEN

Teddy and Karen Wallace sat at a coffee shop three blocks away from Firebrand. Irina had begged him to stay for a drink and he'd almost obliged, but there were more pressing matters at hand. He did, however, promise that he'd be back later that evening and would take her out for a nightcap once her shift ended at ten o'clock.

They'd been there for over an hour. He hated the inaction but they were stuck, and Karen said that a hot cup of coffee always helped clear her thoughts.

Teddy thought that what she meant was a bottomless pot, quiche, and pie. For the past fifteen minutes he'd watched her jot notes down onto a small yellow pad that she'd pulled from the inside pocket of her suit coat. He admitted to himself that while he'd had a crush on her since the day his father had hired her to keep an eye on Sara, his mind, and libido, were now drifting elsewhere.

Irina looked amazing now that she'd gotten herself together. In a strange, roundabout way, down in that place where some thoughts are better left alone, he realized that if someone hadn't threatened Sara's life for a second time, he may never have gone back to Firebrand or crossed paths with Irina again, so this unfortunate situation had some silver lining to it.

And, best of all, now that he could simply admire Karen Wallace for what she was—a strong, beautiful, intelligent partner, rather than an object of desire—it might make their working relationship more efficient.

Right? He wondered if he should mention that to her. Would she appreciate it?

What would his therapist say? Or better yet, what kind of advice would *Sara* give him? She always told it to him straight, whereas sometimes he could sense that his therapist, Dr. Alan Hanks, might be telling him what he wanted to hear. Jim had likely paid the white-haired old kook too well to fit dear little Teddy into his packed schedule. Gotta keep those checks coming, Doc.

Teddy turned it over in his mind.

He could envision Dr. Hanks saying, "Teddy, my boy, the truth is always best, even when it's a lie." Or maybe that was Detective Barker, who was not his biggest fan and had a tendency to spread misinformation just to watch him squirm.

Sara would say, "Teddy, seriously…do you honestly think that Karen Wallace gives a crap about you? Has she sent you any signals of affection whatsoever?" Harsh, true, but Sara had a way of being able to read people like he couldn't.

Was the Sara in his mind right? Did Karen Wallace give a shit?

Probably not.

He took a bite of a cranberry orange scone, grimaced, and said, "Ugh. Why would someone eat this on purpose?"

Without looking up from her notes, Karen smirked and said, "You ordered it."

"Well, yeah, because I thought it sounded good. That tastes like somebody sprayed fruity air freshener on a biscuit."

That got a sympathetic laugh from her.

Teddy washed the last of the bite down with a gulp of chocolate milk. It didn't improve the taste in his mouth at all. Impatient, he said, "Shouldn't we be doing something productive?"

"I am. I'm recreating the scene back at the bar with your posse. Sometimes it helps me to draw a better mental picture if I try to visualize what I might not have seen while I was looking at it."

"Uh…what?" Teddy grabbed her fork and cut away a chunk of her spinach and cheddar quiche.

"What're you doing?"

"Having a bite?"

Karen rolled her eyes and yanked the fork from his hand.

Rude, Teddy thought as she slid her plate out of his reach.

"Pay attention, you might learn something."

"Okay."

"This is what I do. Actually, let me back up a bit." Karen took a sip of her coffee. "Our brains are processing so much—okay, maybe not yours—"

"Hey!"

Karen chuckled. "Kidding. Anyway, our brains process so much that we're not consciously aware of every bit of it, right? I don't know the exact science behind it, but we'd short circuit if we were aware of everything that our brains are processing and taking in at the same time. Make sense? You look confused."

"That's because I am."

"Try it this way. While you're sitting there with a piece of scone on your cheek, you might be looking at me at the same time, and you're aware of seeing me, and you may also be aware of the sensation of something stuck to your cheek, which is when most polite people would take the hint to wipe food off of their faces."

"You're saying I'm aware I have food on my face?"

"You do, but that's not the point."

Teddy swiped at his cheek.

"Other side. Good. Got it."

"I still don't get it, and what does this have to do with Ivan and the guys?"

"The thing I'm trying to get you to see is that even though you see me, you feel the food, and maybe the weight of the fork in your hand, *that's* what you're consciously aware of, but at the same time, your brain is also processing the man in the far corner reading his newspaper. He came in about twenty minutes after we did. His hat is a bit off to one side. You might also be hearing the construction sounds going on outside. You can hear the jackhammer way off in the distance, but it's not really processing because you're focused on what's in front of you. Just because you're not paying attention to it doesn't mean that it's not happening. You might also miss the smell of the waitress's perfume—"

"Oh, no, I got that. Patchouli makes my eyes water."

"Good, that's a start. Anyway, so what I try to do is go into this sort of zone where I recreate the setting in my head and try to pluck out what I might've missed the first time."

"You mean like when you watch *Fight Club* over

and over to pick up on all the spots in the film where Tyler Durden is spliced into a scene?"

"Something like that, yeah. Just think of it as watching a movie over and over and you notice new details each time."

"Got it. That was probably easier than what you were trying to describe."

"Next time I'll start with the caveman explanation first."

It was Teddy's turn to roll his eyes. Half in jest, half offended. He thought, *I wouldn't want to be with someone who treats me like something stuck to the bottom of a shoe anyway, so, uh,* your *loss, Karen.* "Whatever," he said. "So what did your subconscious pick up on back there at the bar? I've known Ivan for years and I don't really think he'd be hiding anything from me."

"He's an ex-Russian mafia boss, Teddy. He'd probably sell Irina to the highest bidder if it came to that. Who, by the way, has the serious hots for you, if you couldn't tell."

"I know. She looks great. Really cleaned herself up." He wasn't interested in talking about Irina, though, because Sara's safety was more important. You know, at least until about ten o'clock that night, and by then she'd be okay and totally out of danger, wouldn't she? It'd be cool to hang out with Irina *then*, right?

Teddy asked, "Do you think Ivan was hiding something from us?"

Karen shook her head and scanned her notes again. "Not him. He might've been right when he said that the Spirit finds you, but that other guy, Viktor, I'm pretty sure I saw him shake his head when Ivan mentioned it."

Teddy cocked his head and tried to replay the scene in his mind, the way Karen had. "Wait, yeah, now that you mention it…he shook his head and took a sip of whiskey right after that, didn't he?"

"Nice! Yeah, and it looked to me like he was trying to hide it. Viktor knows something. He may not know exactly where the Spirit is, but he's got information."

"So do you want to go back there to talk to him?"

Karen shook her head. "Not a chance he'd reveal anything in front of Ivan or his comrades. He'd lose the trust they've all worked on for fifty years. But…we could stake it out and wait on him to go home. He's gotta go home at some point, doesn't he?"

Teddy fiddled with the saltshaker between his fingers. "I've seen that guy pull all-nighters, sometimes two or three days in a row. He and Ivan, and Andrei, are superhuman once they get a good game of Hold 'em running. We could be waiting until next week."

"Damn."

"I couldn't hang with them. They were brutal. "

"What if… Yeah, maybe that'd work. How close is your girlfriend to the rest of those guys?"

"Who? Irina?"

"Yeah."

"Very." Teddy faked a horrible Russian accent. "In Mother Russia, family is strong like bull, even when not family."

"You're ridiculous."

"I know."

"What if she's more into *you* than her grandfather's old cronies? Love tears families apart sometimes. I saw the way she looked at you."

"Maybe, but what're we talking about here?"

"All I want you to do is call Irina and ask her to keep an eye on Viktor. Try to eavesdrop on any phone conversations he might have if she's around. Oh, and especially if he leaves. You said he rarely leaves if they're on a bender, right? It'd be awfully convenient if he left right after we did."

"We left, what, an hour and ten minutes ago? What if he's already gone?"

Karen considered the possibility. "Nah, if Viktor's got anything to hide about an enemy of Ivan's, then he won't risk making a move so soon. He'd have to make it look natural."

"Good point."

"But you should probably call soon, just in case."

"You think it's safe to now?"

"Go for it."

Teddy got up from the table and walked to the far corner of the café, dialing Firebrand's number as he went. Irina picked up immediately, answering in her cute, Russian cowgirl accent. Teddy whispered, asking her not to reveal anything in case Oleg remained at the bar. Close by, he noticed the elderly gentlemen give him an obvious glance. It wasn't much, but enough to insinuate, "You're too close. Move."

Personal space…yet another concept he and his therapist were working on. What was the standard etiquette for U.S. citizens? Something like three feet? Was that what Dr. Hanks had said? In European countries it was more like inches.

Regardless, Teddy smiled at the man and moved twelve inches away while he relayed his instructions to Irina.

As Karen had surmised, Irina was thrilled to help Teddy, saying, "He's my least favorite, so y'all do whatever you need to, *compadre*."

He said goodbye, and considered asking Irina to keep using the cowgirl accent when they were out later. That might be fun.

Karen finished her last bite of quiche as Teddy sat down with a huge grin. She asked, "Are we good to go?"

"I could hear her smiling through the phone, so yeah, she's in."

"Did you tell her why? You didn't say a word about me bring a P.I., did you? Because we don't know how well that would fly with—"

Teddy put his hand across the table and patted her arm. "*Chill*, dude. I'm not the idiot everyone thinks I am, okay?"

She grinned. "I'll take that under consideration. So was Viktor still there?"

"As far as she knew, yeah. There's a back entrance that she can't quite keep an eye on, but she said that ninety percent of the time he'll leave through the front so he can grab a beer for the road."

"Upstanding citizen."

"Well, he's not Mother Theresa. She's supposed to call if he leaves anytime soon, but if it starts getting busy, which it likely will around five o'clock, we're on our own."

"Good enough."

"So what's next? Do we keep following leads or go ask around at the places you were talking about earlier? What's the plan?"

"Teddy, put the caffeine away. We wait."

"For what?"

"I know you think I have some sort of exciting job filled with binoculars and lasers and shootouts, but a huge part of being a private investigator is sitting, and waiting, and observing. It's a slow process sometimes. I've waited *days* to capture the right photograph. I sit in my car and drink coffee at all hours of the night, hoping that some guy's wife will leave her lover's apartment so I can take a picture and go home. It can be mind numbing, but when all you have is a flimsy lead and a strong hunch, you ride it out until the option is gone."

"Yeah, but Sara may not have days for us to wait. What if we're totally off about Viktor and he wasn't subconsciously signaling that he knew something about the Spirit, huh? We need to be proactive, not reactive."

"How, Teddy? Where do you suggest we go?"

"Your places—the churches, the markets, whatever, the ones where you said you knew some of the Russian immigrants. What if somebody there knows him?"

"First, that was a long shot because I didn't know where else to start. Second, if any of them knows where he is, there's a good chance that they'd be too terrified of him to say anything, or, if he's family, they'll keep their mouths shut to protect him. You brought us to the right place, Teddy. Thank God you had this weird little connection, because otherwise we'd be spinning in circles and chasing dead or fake leads. I know you're worried about Sara, but our best bet is to wait a while. Who knows, maybe Viktor sent a text message when we weren't looking and the Spirit will find *us*, just like Ivan said."

"I'm not sure Viktor knows what a text is. He's still struggling with the fact that phones don't hang on walls anymore. But really, do we want this Spirit guy to find us? What if he's…dangerous?"

"Then you'll be able to tell Irina about how brave you were."

Teddy heard an unfamiliar voice over his shoulder. "I'm too old to be dangerous. Move over so I can sit."

Teddy felt the gun barrel placed discreetly against his side before Karen spotted it.

SEVENTEEN

Quirk sat with Boudica in the visitors' room of the Coffee Creek Correctional Facility.

It smelled like old perfume, bad coffee, and despair.

On their side of the glass, families gathered around telephones attached to stalls and talked to their loved—and incarcerated—ones on the other side. Some smiled, some laughed, all regretted that things had to be this way. A mother consoled her daughter, who, admittedly, looked good in the orange jumpsuit. Quirk noticed that it really brought out the shine in her greasy, uncombed blonde hair.

The mother was saying something about a boy named Brayden and how much he'd grown over the past year, and that he loved preschool. The daughter put her hand on the thick glass and tried to fight back the tears. She didn't succeed.

Being there, standing inside a prison, wasn't the best idea, in his opinion, but according to the woman controlling his every move, hiding in plain sight was clearly a preferable option. "You cover your ass well enough, you can stay as free as long as you like. Just don't get your picture on the boob tube, because that's when it all goes downhill. This way," she'd said as they walked inside the prison visitors' entrance, "you get to breathe. I'd rather live as a criminal outside than hide in some dungeon a free woman."

It made sense, Quirk thought, as he stood there with her awaiting their turn. However, what she'd failed to mention, or forgotten about, was the potential of their faces on the streetview cams around Portland. He recalled that was how they got leads on the Boston Marathon bombers. The two pricks carrying their backpacks in full view, unafraid. Regardless of what happened after Boudica's planned event, he hoped he wouldn't see himself on the nightly news sprinting away from the parking garage, ready to piss his pants.

Boudica said, "There she comes," and pointed at a young woman. "A friend of Sara Winthrop's."

To Quirk, her wink and mischievous smile suggested that the word "friend" was far from accurate.

The guard led them to an empty stall and was kind enough to pull out the seat for Boudica. He called her ma'am, and Quirk thought, *If the guy only knew.*

The young woman across from them, sitting with her ankles and wrists chained together, looked haggard, hardened, and empty.

She'd been beautiful at some point in the past. Quirk could see it…at least on one side of her face. On the other side, her cheek was ragged and mottled, faded red valleys carved into it as a result of scarring and poor stitching. The missing upper half of her left ear had the distinct shape of a bite mark, the way a surfboard looks when a hungry shark gets a mouthful of fiberglass and leg.

The scarring extended down to her neck on the left side and tracing perpendicular across that was another, thinner scar that went from beneath one ear, around her throat, and up to the other ear.

She wore an eye patch, too, and Quirk had no desire to see what was behind it.

The young woman picked up the phone, held it to her ear, and waited.

Boudica said, "Hi, Shelley," holding the phone so that Quirk could hear as well.

"Who are you?" she asked with no hint of care, or emotion, or actual curiosity, almost as if she were on autopilot. Her voice was ragged and raspy. "I'm not doing any more interviews, if that's what you're here for. Actually, here's a quote for you—Sara Winthrop can go die in a fire. I don't care anymore."

Boudica had refused to reveal her little surprise as they'd driven to Coffee Creek, and now that they were here, with Shelley sitting in front of them, Quirk felt the fog of confusion lift. Sara Winthrop, their—or *Boudica's*—intended target, had survived and saved her children from a horrific, sadistic kidnapping. It'd been all over the news a year and a half ago. He remembered now.

Boudica said, "We're friends of yours."

"I don't know you."

"Not now, but you will."

Shelley laughed. "You think so, huh?"

Quirk remembered more as Boudica made small talk about the food and the showers.

A detective had died trying to help and then there were follow-up stories about how the female inmates of Coffee Creek, many of them mothers themselves, had responded to the new inmate—one who'd dared to use children in her evil plans. There'd been a small riot; the warden barely contained it and saved an inmate's life. The warden, when it was all over, had said something to the effect of, "She's alive, but from the looks of it, she'll wish she was dead."

He remembered. Why, he didn't know, but he remembered. It was big news back then. A Portland mother, fighting back against her attackers and winning—what wasn't there to love about that story? And then the villainess got her comeuppance in prison at the hands of a horde of angry mothers—he remembered thinking that off camera the news anchors were probably high fiving and saluting the retribution.

Unbelievable. This was the young woman that had started the job, and now Boudica wanted to finish it for her.

And Sara Winthrop—the target—why her? Quirk remembered admiring the woman for her resolve, watching the story on the news as he assembled their first bomb meant for Moscow.

As he sat listening to Boudica and this young woman, a feeling rose within him—a notion that the façade Boudica presented regarding their cause was false, that what they were fighting was a *personal* war for *her*, not to spread awareness of the severity of video game violence.

What had Boudica said earlier? That the *real* target in London had been someone outside of the video game shop? Was Sara the real target behind their planned bombing in Portland? What about Beijing, Rio, and Moscow? Had he and Cleo, Tank and Rocket, Chief and Sharkfin…had they all been led astray by this woman?

If so, what would he do about it?

Anything? Did he have a choice?

If Boudica had been betraying them for close to eighteen months now, did it matter if he kept his mouth shut for a couple more, long enough to finish here, to finish in Paris, and be done? Maybe it didn't. Maybe it did. All this sweat, stress, and fear—Cleo's death, the FBI's involvement, all those people hurt by the bombs he'd built…was it all for nothing? A worthless waste of time?

Not necessarily. Even if Boudica had tricked their little team into congregating under false pretenses, even if she'd been fighting for something different, people were talking. The media had begun to take notice, especially after the destruction in London. After The Clan had claimed London and voiced their reason behind it, various experts had been asked to offer their opinions on shows like Anderson Cooper's and Nancy Grace's. Some for, some against. Some saying there was no correlation whatsoever and that there were studies to prove it. Quirk knew better. All those studies denouncing the connections, they didn't mean a damn thing. He knew they were wrong. He'd seen it firsthand and—

"Quirk?"

He blinked and refocused. Boudica smiled at him. "What?" he said.

"I was just telling Shelley here what a caring

person you are and how you helped put that poor, sick dog out of its misery."

Quirk dipped his eyebrows and cocked an ear toward her. "Dog?"

"Cleo was such a good dog, wasn't she? Such a shame that we had to help her cross over."

He felt a corner of his upper lip turn up in disgust, but decided he needed to play along. For now. Boudica knew too much about him. His plans, his hopes, his movements. If he pissed her off, the Spirit might show up sooner than expected. Quirk said, "Yeah, damn shame. Pretty dog, too."

Also, he had assumed that Boudica wouldn't allow him to live beyond their final objective, thus the contingency plans he had in place. In theory, he could leave tomorrow. What was keeping him? Why not disappear now before she had a chance to suspect something was wrong? She'd already had her suspicions anyway; what was there to say that she wouldn't send in the Spirit simply for posterity?

And as much as he hated to acknowledge the fact about himself, greed was an identifiable culprit for his delay. He'd already saved enough to send his former sister-in-law, Melissa, a sizeable safety net—anonymously donated by a shell charity he would establish, of course—which left him with barely what he needed to disappear.

The fact was, when it came to money used to start a new life as someone else, more was always better.

He need the funds and *had* a cause to fight for, even if Boudica was deceitfully fighting for something else.

Stay. Endure. Escape.

Three simple steps, no more, no less, bridged by building one more bomb, supposing that was all Boudica had in mind. Was the one in his basement meant for Sara Winthrop now, as it had been before? She'd told him about the detonation at the Winthrops' house and Sara's survival, and he knew it wouldn't be long before the bomb technicians and forensics teams would be piecing together the puzzle of his contraption.

He'd worked hard on not having any defining signature as a bomb maker, to remain a chameleon, but still, if they were good enough, there would always be the chance of him making a mistake. He had confidence in his abilities, but the universe often squashed confidence like an egg under an anvil.

Boudica said to Shelley, "You're probably wondering why we're here."

So am I, Quirk thought. He hadn't entirely been listening the whole time, but up to that point, it merely seemed like Boudica had ran into a distant friend at a cocktail party.

Shelley said, "I mean, yeah, hey, it's fun talking to you and all, even though I have no clue who you are, but as soon as I walk out of here, it's time for my daily abuse in the showers. Give me a real reason to walk in there with a smile on my face."

"First," Boudica whispered as she leaned closer to the window, "we're going to finish what you started. I know you tried, and you got damn close, but I'm glad you didn't, because you would've fucked up what I've been planning for the past twenty years. I want the pleasure of watching Sara Winthrop burn."

Shelley drummed her fingers on the table and offered a limp smile. "More power to you. Send me a postcard when you're done."

The guard at the door behind them raised his voice. "Hands and heads where I can see them, please. Thank you."

Boudica leaned back away from the window. Still whispering, but so quietly she was almost mouthing the words, she added, "Second, I like you. I like your spirit. You've got some spunk, but you're minor league, honey. How much longer you got in here?"

Shelley shrugged. "After time off for good behavior, I might get out in time to buy my own casket."

"What if I told you there were strings to pull?"

"I'd say keep dreaming."

"And if I were serious?"

"I'd ask you to give me some of whatever you're smoking."

"Two years. You stay patient for two more years. Sit in there like a good little girl should, but you take that time to let all that anger build up inside you. Poke it, stab it, make it bleed. You look hollow, Shelley. Fill yourself up with every bit of rage you can imagine. Don't waste it on Sara Winthrop. That's my job. Two years should be enough to get you close to detonation. After that, you come work for me. We'll make the world afraid of us."

Quirk watched as Shelley listened. She took it in, but Quirk couldn't be sure that she was buying it. If she was, then the quiet way in which she received it was nearly as disturbing as if she'd jumped on the table and shouted, "Hallelujah!"

So they were on a recruiting mission, huh? That's what this was about.

Did Boudica intend for Shelley Sergeant to replace Cleo in The Clan?

Hell, why not? There were worse ideas. He wasn't so sure that letting Shelley Sergeant fester in prison for two more years, before she somehow magically freed her, was the best idea, but then again, he wouldn't be around to find out. Physically. As in, on the other side of the world. Not "wouldn't be around" meaning "dead."

Quirk felt a bead of sweat trickle down his side. It was cold against his skin.

He shivered.

Could've been the sweat.

Could've been the insane grin that passed across Shelley Sergeant's lips when Boudica told her that the world wouldn't be ready for them.

Either way, he was thankful that she was on the other side of the bars for another two years.

EIGHTEEN

Sara cautiously kept an eye on the two unfamiliar men while she waited on Barker. In the backseat, her children were scrunched in along with Miss Willow. The mom instinct took over, and she questioned the safety of no child seats in the back of Barker's unmarked sedan. Safety first, but it seemed nearly inconsequential considering the fact that their home had been reduced to smoldering rubble in a murderous attempt.

Who had called her house and warned Miss Willow? And my God, what if she hadn't answered the phone in order to heed the warning? Sara thought about the possibility of having to identify her family by their remains, gagged on the bile in the back of her throat, and then swallowed the vile taste.

She listened to the kids bicker in the back seat, clambering over one another to get a better view of their destroyed home. To them it was this massive, unbelievable occurrence, almost *cool* in a way. Explosions, smoke, fire, ambulances, police, sirens and lights, it certainly didn't happen every day, and it certainly didn't happen on their street. They'd mentioned the loss of a few things, like toys and clothes. Jacob felt sad about his goldfish, but otherwise, it was mostly, "Look how far that water is spraying!" and, "Did you see that policeman's gun?" and, "Those fire trucks sure are big!"

The final question, the innocent one that sent Sara reeling—as if the rest of it hadn't—was a simple, "Mom, when we get a new place, can I have my own room?"

Sara snapped. "Lacey, stop it. Our house is still burning, and you're already talking about the next one."

"I just wanted—"

"*No*, not right now." Sara leaned forward, elbows on her knees, and rested her head in her hands. They smelled like dirty asphalt. Disgusting, but it was better than looking at her ruined past outside the car windows. In a way, though, maybe Lacey had the right idea.

She was free to look ahead to the future.

That house had held plenty of good memories, but a lot of bad ones were associated with it as well. She'd lost keepsakes and photo albums. First locks of hair and bronzed baby shoes. Her old wedding dress that had meant something long before Brian had disappeared. The mugs that her grandmother had given her were likely gone, as were the two-hundred-year-old picture frames that had been handed down as wedding gifts through her family.

All of her past, obliterated, except for some minor, salvageable items.

The absence of the house didn't eradicate the bad memories, but it surely couldn't hurt to finally be free of the place where she'd spent so many agonizing nights. That house had been associated with Brian's disappearance—two years of holding her breath and waiting. Shelley Sergeant had been inside as well, tainting what good energy remained. There were days and nights spent inside those walls, dealing with all the post-trauma things after she'd rescued her children.

It was rather morbid to think of it this way, because she had been so close to losing everything, again, but if Patty Kellog was behind this, then maybe she'd inadvertently done Sara a favor. The evil wench had wiped part of the slate clean.

Barker interrupted her train of thought when he climbed in the car. He ran his fingers through his wet white hair. "I've been here twenty years," he said, "and I don't think I'll ever get used to this rain. Anyway, they're treating it as an attempted homicide, of course, along with a whole other host of options—basically whatever they can pile on if they catch who did it."

"Well, we *know* who, right?"

"They still have to go through the process, but I gave them a heads-up about our meeting with Timms. I had to fight them for it, but I got clearance to get you and the young 'uns to a safe place—Jim's, like you said—but they'll have to come by later for some questioning."

"Just get us away from here. I'm sick of looking at it."

Barker nodded, said something encouraging to the kids and Miss Willow, and then gave Sara a pitiful look.

"What?"

"Nothing."

"What, Barker?"

"I'm sorry, that's all. This is—it's almost too much, even for me. Before you say it, I know…I've still got a home to go to and people aren't trying to murder me, at least not today, but you've got heart, and I want you to keep it that way. Don't let shit like this—sorry, kids—don't let crap like this get you down. Those aren't the most comforting words—"

"Barker! My house exploded!"

"I'm not good at this stuff, Sara, but you know what I mean, don't you?"

He was trying, and Sara couldn't fault him for that. She slumped in her seat, annoyed but thankful for his pitiable attempt. "I shouldn't have yelled at you. I'm... This is insane. Can we get out of here? Now? Please?"

"Yes, ma'am." His cell phone rang on his belt before he could turn the ignition key. The noise reminded Sara of the old one in the house where she grew up with the yellow linoleum and paneled walls. She expected to glance down and see a 1980s rotary dial phone strapped to his hip. He checked the ID and said, "Hang on a sec, let me see what this is all about."

Sara leaned over the front seat and shushed the kids, whispering for them to get buckled in as best as they could. Miss Willow sat in the middle with the twins to her right and Jacob to her left. She couldn't stop staring at the house and shaking her head.

Beside Sara, Barker mumbled, "Uh-huh, right...no...that's a damn shame. Who's on it? Good, good. Wait, who was the girl?"

Sara said to Miss Willow, "You okay?"

"No," she answered, trying to hold back a sob. "I just keep thinking about what might've happened if I hadn't answered the phone. I mean, I don't know whether it was luck, chance, or fate. We were so close to...I can't even say it."

Sara reached over the seat. "Here, give me your hand." Miss Willow lifted a shaky hand and Sara took it, squeezing. "We can't mold the past to fit the future,

Willow, and all we can do is shake our fist at the sky or hold up our hands in praise. Either way, you made the right choice. It doesn't matter what influenced it. You did it, and here we are. You saved their lives."

Miss Willow managed a grin and pushed a loose strand of long gray hair behind her ear. She dabbed at her nose with a tissue. "I suppose."

Sara squeezed her hand once more and returned her attention to Barker. He continued to ask questions for another five minutes, seemingly growing more and more agitated as time passed. He hung up and sat staring blankly out the window at her house. He chewed a cinnamon toothpick like he was angry at it, grabbed the tip, and then slung it to the floorboard of his car.

"Everything okay?" Sara asked. With so much going on around them outside of Barker's sedan, where they were securely ensconced inside their little realm of safety, she wondered what could've possibly upset him that much. There were sirens and shouts from patrolmen urging the crowd to back away. Firemen spraying fat streams onto the smoldering ruins. It looked like a couple of plain-clothes detectives had arrived in addition to the medical examiner. Oh, and now the news vans with their antennas and beautiful reporters with their perfectly coiffed hair and false sincerity. Wonderful.

And still the two men stealing occasional glances at her remained in the crowd. Was it enough to be afraid of them, or were they curious because someone had told them it was her home sitting over there like a burning trash heap?

"What happened?" she asked.

"Remember how Timms blasted out of LightPulse like a cat with its tail on fire?"

"Yeah."

Barker lowered his voice and leaned closer to Sara, motioning for her to come nearer with his hand. "I can't say it in front of the kids."

"Is he okay?" she whispered.

"They're zipping up the body bag right now."

Sara gasped and recoiled. From the backseat, Miss Willow asked what was going on. "Nothing, Willow—just keep them distracted, please?" To Barker, she said, "What—was it an accident?"

Barker started the car, turned up the radio, and then deftly maneuvered through the sea of emergency vehicles. "Not unless he tripped and fell onto a bullet moving faster than the speed of sound."

Sara risked a peek to her right and watched the unfamiliar men pretend to ignore her exit. Gawkers? Ambulance chasers? Was that it? Were they lawyers looking for a quick scheme? That actually made sense. Satisfied they were harmless, she said, "Timms was *murdered*?"

"Yep, looks that way. They found him in the bottom floor of a parking garage." They were in the clear now, driving past rows of houses with distant neighbors standing on their porches, hiding under umbrellas or overhangs, watching the commotion down the street. "Initially, they were suspecting murder-suicide because there's another body there with him but no weapon. Young woman. One of the patrol boys recognized her, and from the way it sounds, they think it might've been that Emily gal that he was on the phone with before he left. They've got some FBI jerkoffs there now trying to take over the scene and everybody's jockeying for position, but murder's at the state level, not federal. I'm sure they'll figure out how to wrestle it away from the locals somehow."

"So who was Emily?"

"Are you ready for this?"

"No, but go ahead."

"Tolson—he's a good guy, I think you'd like him—Tolson managed to get some info from one of the squares. Guy tells him that Timms had been working with this young lady, trying to bring down a clan…only the guy doesn't know it's actually called *The* Clan, right? Word was, Timms had been bragging about turning and burning the poor thing."

Sara checked her rearview mirror, gut instinct insisting that she needed to be cautious. She wasn't sure if she'd even be able to identify someone following them regardless. In the backseat, Miss Willow was doing a perfect job entertaining the kids with I-Spy. Sara said, "I don't know what that means."

"Right. Um, well, he'd turned her, as in, she was a member of Kellog's Clan that had turned snitch—"

"Whoa, that's how he knew so much about Patty and her history with the bombings."

"Exactly."

"And what does burning her mean?"

"It's stupid."

"What? Tell me."

"Turn and burn…trust me, this is all speculation, because I've never actually used or been privy to the term myself, but 'turn and burn' means to flip the contact and then sleep with her."

"You're serious? How does 'burn' mean sex with a witness?"

"Use a rubber…burn rubber…burn. Turn and burn."

"I don't—forget it. I don't want to know. So

Timms is sleeping with someone that was part of Patty Kellog's Clan—"

"Cleo, I think it was."

"Cleo, and he's pumping her for information—oh God, I didn't mean it like that—that was horrible. He manages to get her to reveal plans about Chicago and Portland…and about Paris. Patty blatantly told the FBI that her next target was Chicago, but turning Cleo was how he knew that *I'm* the target *here*, instead."

"Sounds about right, Detective Winthrop."

"So why were Cleo and Timms meeting in the sub-level of a garage downtown?"

"I wouldn't put money on it, but maybe they got together to burn rubber."

Sara scoffed. "Not after the way he sprinted out of the office. You saw how freaked out he was."

"That's why I wouldn't put money on it. Remember what he said in Jim's office when he took that call? *Cleo*, I'm assuming, had somebody else held hostage, for lack of a better term, and Timms was late for their rendezvous. Something happened on the other end of that phone call, because he didn't get panicked until he couldn't get a response from her."

"That's right," Sara said. "Turn here." She knew that Barker had a vague idea about how to get to Jim Rutherford's house up in the hills of Portland, but his quick signal and taking the curve on two wheels showed a lack of recollection. "So what does that tell us?"

"The way I see it, Cleo has somebody she wants Timms to meet, maybe another informant, who knows. Timms is late to their meetup because he took too long swinging his pecker in our faces, he gets the call, and then panics when something happens—that *something*, I'm guessing, is their mystery guest escaping or fighting back against Cleo. Timms gets to the rally point, sees Cleo dead or dying, and then gets whacked when his back is turned."

Sara said, "Left here and go up about three blocks, then another right," then asked, "So do we think it's the mystery guest that shot both of them? Wait, were they both *shot*?"

Barker nodded. "Double-tap to the female vic's chest, one behind Timms's left ear, and *no*, actually, they don't think it was the same weapon. Tolson said they appear to be two different types of entry and exit wounds, but that doesn't mean that our mystery person didn't have two different weapons on him."

"How do we know it was a him?"

"We don't, but statistically, violence this…well…*violent* is relegated to the male of the species."

"You *do* remember Shelley Sergeant, right?" Sara noticed Jim's street sailing past out the window. "You missed it, Barker. We should've made a right on Bellingham."

"I wouldn't say I missed it," he said, looking in the rearview mirror. "I'm taking the scenic route."

"Why? We need to get to Jim's."

"We will, but first I want to see if our friend back there thinks he's going to the same place."

"Who?"

"Blue Dodge Ram, the one with the camper top about three cars back. He's been with us since about two blocks from your house. Not that I'm entirely suspicious…just being cautious, that's all."

Sara's stomach churned. She realized he had a reason to be wary.

NINETEEN

Teddy whimpered. It was subtle and emasculating, but it was there, and he prayed that neither the old man nor Karen had heard it. If the old man was the Spirit, he didn't want to show fear. Could bad guys smell fear like dogs? Teddy hoped not.

Plus, he wanted Karen to know he could be brave.

Before the insanity with Shelly Sergeant and nearly losing his life at the hands of her brother, Michael, he'd been confident and poised. He'd never met a stranger. Granted, according to Sara, and Dr. Hanks, this self-assuredness had the tendency to be overbearing and annoying to stranger, friend, and coworker alike, but that was Teddy Rutherford.

Capital T, Capital R.

To the outside world, he was fairly close to being the pre-Shelley Teddy that everyone loved and adored. Or, well, tolerated and accepted. But on the inside, he'd been a quivering mess for months.

It had begun with the dream. Night after night. He was back in the cabin, and instead of Sara inside the cage, he was trapped within the small, metallic walls.

Naked, chained, and helpless, but not fearful. Not yet.

Candles burned. A sweet smell like fresh doughnuts wafted through the room.

Michael, the monstrous creature, was nowhere to be seen. Instead, Shelley Sergeant sat outside his cage. Beautiful, smiling, and also nude, with her hands crossed neatly in her lap. She seemed shy, almost. He sat patiently, longingly staring at her perfect breasts—perfection that only nature can provide. Flawless skin. Hair up. He could feel the warmth growing between his legs. And then…

It was the same dream. Always. He thought they were involved in some sort of freaky sub-dom sex game, like, "Oh, the dog cage would be fun, let's try that," or, "Okay, sweetie, it's your turn to get in this time."

Every night, in every dream, Shelley's smile would disappear and be replaced by rows of stalactite and stalagmite fangs dripping with saliva. Her eyes would disappear only to be replaced by empty sockets of the darkest depths of blackness. She would stand and reveal the glory of her perfect body and he would feel himself getting aroused in spite of his fear and her hideous face.

Next came the torture. Hot pokers pulled from the

flaming fireplace. Cattle prods. Spears. Anything that Shelley the she-beast could find to jab, burn, and cut him with while he was trapped inside that godawful cage. He'd cry out, and in the final moments of his life the door to the cabin would swing open, casting a bright, warm light inside.

But he always woke up. He never got to learn whether he lived or died.

Dr. Hanks suggested that he was possibly dealing with some post-traumatic stress while his brain worked through the issues. In time, and with the proper medication, the dreams would stop. Or, on the other hand, his subconscious issues could merely signify that he was feeling trapped in life and his career and the horrible nightmare was how his mind chose to process the external information.

Teddy feared that it was a premonition that someday Shelley would come back to finish what she started. Now, however, if things continued on their current path, someone, this Boudica person, would beat her to the finale.

The dream, if it *was* a moment of precognitive foresight, never mentioned the fact that he might die after having had a cranberry orange scone as his final meal.

He hated being weak, but with a gun at his side,

did he have an option?

To his left the old man coughed, removed a white handkerchief from a jacket pocket, and blew his nose, then coughed again. Teddy squirmed uneasily in his seat. He wasn't sure how steady those feeble hands were. One hearty cough, a twitchy finger, and wind would whistle through his insides.

Karen noticed the small, snub-nosed pistol in his hand. She said, "Hey, why don't you put that away? We're all friends here, right?"

"No."

She said, "What's your name?"

Come on, Karen, Teddy thought, yo*u know exactly who it is. You don't find the Spirit, the Spirit finds you*. Teddy shifted in his seat again. The barrel dug deeper into his side.

"Vadim Bariskov, madam, also known as the Spirit. Also known as The Red Death, or, here in your homeland, you may have heard another name. Does the codename 'Dark Horse' mean anything to you?"

It meant nothing to Teddy except for the fact that this schizophrenic Russian death machine could put a bullet in him using any name he wanted. He noticed that Karen leaned forward with her elbows on the table, mouth agape, with her hands on each cheek. "Some of the spooks I knew used to tell stories about

Dark Horse that were just as crazy as the stories about the Spirit. You're…that's all *you*?"

Bariskov smiled, showing crooked, yellow teeth. "I am three in one. You don't need St. Peter to introduce you to the Father, Son, and Holy *Spirit*, eh? Huh?" He laughed. "I'm sitting right here in front of you. Come now, confess your sins."

"You're Dark Horse?"

Bariskov's accent disappeared. "Sweetheart, I've been playing both sides since Junior here was going poo-poo in the diaper." He squeezed Teddy's neck playfully and then pulled the gun away from his ribs. "I won't forget where this is, no? Let's talk," he said, and then tucked it inside his jacket.

Teddy said, "So are you Russian or American?"

Bariskov took a bite of Teddy's scone, chewed slowly, and swallowed. He said, in an accent that wobbled between Long Island and the Kremlin, "Am I American? Am I Russian?" Then he switched to faultless French. "*Oui*, do I come from Paris?" Texas now. "Or do I come from Dallas, y'all?" His final accent, which seemed to be the one with which he was most familiar, was the original Russian, overlaid with a number of years living in the States. "Does not matter, Mr. Rutherford. I come, I go. I am the Spirit. I walk through a wall in Portland, I show up in Sweden. It's all the same to me. He pays me, she pays me. Today she pays me to kill him, tomorrow she dies because he paid more. All the same."

Karen appeared to be in awe, but slightly fearful. Teddy assumed that the Spirit—or The Red Death, or Dark Horse, or whoever this guy claimed to be—had a mythical reputation within Karen's former circles. She said, "I can't believe you're sitting right here. Do you know what the bounty was on your head?"

"One million, or so I've heard. Small potatoes, my dear. If you're looking to claim it, consider sparing an old man's life, eh? Huh? I can tell you how to find five more criminals worth just as much if that's what you're after."

Karen shook her head. "No, no, that's not what I meant. I mean, you're…*here*," she said, shoving her mug to the side. "No one back in my old office would ever believe me."

Bariskov winked. "I'd rather not test that theory. So, my friends," he said, ruffling Teddy's hair, "Viktor tells me you're interested in finding the Spirit. Well, now you have him. What's on your mind?"

Teddy had no doubt that Bariskov could eliminate everyone in the café with a flick of his highly trained assassin's wrist, which was probably why Karen had kept her distance and had kept her hands visible. That made sense. She knew him and knew what he was capable of, while Teddy could do nothing but ponder why this fabled international assassin was chatting with them like Grandpa out for coffee.

Teddy slid the cranberry orange scone remnants in front of Bariskov. A peace offering. A steak to appease the hungry lion. And, if the old man actually enjoyed it, it could be called a bribe. As long as it kept Bariskov smiling, that was all that mattered.

Karen said, "I'm Karen Wallace and this is Teddy Rutherford."

"You shouldn't have done that."

Teddy nervously nudged himself away from Bariskov, looking at him sideways, asking, "W-w-why? Why shouldn't she have done that?"

"Names beget death. Always true, Teddy Rutherford. Always true."

"How solid is *always*?"

Bariskov slapped the table and howled with laughter, which then disintegrated into an epic coughing fit. He removed the white hankie from a pocket then hacked into it until the blotchy colors of his face matched the color of the cranberries on the plate.

Teddy offered him some water. Bariskov refused. Instead he removed a flask from his jacket, took a long swig, and tucked it away.

Bariskov said, "Apologies. I'm not the—how do you say—the war machine I once was. Now I'm lucky if I can piss without it feeling like fire in my dick."

Teddy wondered if that bit of information was necessary, but he wasn't about to question it.

Karen said, "We're working a case for a friend of ours and we think you might be associated with it in some small way." Karen lifted her left arm, flashing him her 9mm held in her right hand flat against the table.

Holy shit, Teddy thought. *When did that get there?*

The move surprised Bariskov, as well. He nodded. "Twenty years ago, if you pulled that on the Spirit, you would be dead before your finger touched the trigger."

Karen didn't budge.

Teddy said, "Look, maybe we should just—"

"Teddy?"

"What?"

"Quiet, please." She never broke eye contact with Bariskov.

"Yes, ma'am."

Bariskov said, "Come now, put that away. It's not necessary. I came because Viktor called and said you're looking for the Spirit, and that the woman is pretty, so I should come. Also, as a favor to him because he likes

Teddy. But Viktor and I will need to have a small discussion, because Viktor said nothing about guns and danger."

Karen smirked. "Bullshit. You haven't survived this long by being an idiot. You knew you were walking into something. Why'd you come?"

Teddy could do nothing but watch the banter. Karen and Bariskov were used to this sort of—what was it, espionage? As much as he hated to admit it, this type of mental and verbal sparring was well out of his comfort zone.

"As a favor to Viktor, like I said."

This one Teddy could handle. "But Viktor knows you and Ivan are enemies, right? He wouldn't risk pissing off Ivan."

"My business with the great and mighty Ivan is none of your concern. It is what it is. But you—you and Karen are here for something else. What I can tell you is this: My part is finished, and because of me, Sara Winthrop's children are alive and safe."

Karen squinted and shook her head. "What does that mean?"

"Because I have gotten soft in my old age, they were not present when a place, shall we say, ceased to exist."

"What in the hell are you talking about?"

Bariskov shifted his eyes around the café. Two women carrying rolled up yoga mats, hair up in ponytails, stood at the counter. In the far corner an elderly couple sipped their coffees and read the newspaper. He leaned over the table.

Teddy could smell aftershave and a hint of peppermint coming from the Spirit.

Bariskov said, "This Boudica, she's an amateur. Harsh and dirty. Thirty years ago she would've pissed off the wrong person and would've been long dead before she ever got to where she is now. She works like a hammer beating a nail. It's crude. There's no style or finesse."

Karen said, "So?"

"I don't like her. She's a brute."

"Then why work for her?"

Bariskov rubbed this thumb and forefinger together. "Money. I like it, and she has connections that pay very, very well. But this time she went too far. I'm old and soft. I don't agree with harming children."

Teddy felt his pulse speed up and his cheeks grow warm. He said, "Whoa, what?"

Bariskov held up a wrinkled, liver-spotted hand. "Not to worry, Teddy Rutherford, I spared the family. I warned them, they got out, then I told Dimitri to go ahead. There's no need to worry now."

"Go ahead with what?" Karen asked.

"Let's just say the Winthrop house is no more."

Karen left the 9mm flat against the table, slid it around, and angled the barrel at Bariskov. "And Sara? What about her?"

"I don't know."

"Bullshit."

"On my honor, I don't know. This Boudica, she only calls to give single directions, but I believe I can find out for you."

Teddy sat upright, excited, and nudged closer to Bariskov. "Well, great, that's awesome! So what happens next? Do we just hang around and wait on you to make some phone calls?"

Neither Karen nor Bariskov acknowledged him.

Karen said, "How much do you want?"

Bariskov shook his head. "It's not how much. It's *who*."

TWENTY

On the way back from Coffee Creek and their visit with the vicious-looking Shelley Sergeant, Quirk sat in the passenger's seat while Boudica navigated the rain-soaked interstate. She'd taken the keys from him in the parking lot, saying he drove like her grandmother and she didn't have the time or the patience to watch him creep along.

It was okay by him. With his hands free, there was the possibility of escape, or even taking Boudica out if the desire was strong enough.

She drove in silence while he imagined scenarios of freeing himself from her…what? Her grasp? Her control over him? Her ability to scare him into submission?

Quirk sat with his arms crossed, staring ahead, watching the spray fly up from the interstate and pepper the windshield. He knew that, ultimately, Boudica would likely attempt to kill him once their job in Paris was complete. Also, he wasn't perfectly confident that she wouldn't slit his throat or poison him within the next few hours once they'd taken care of Sara Winthrop.

Man's inherent survival instinct can be a powerful motivator.

New plan. He needed to convince Boudica he was worth keeping around, at least long enough to finish the job in Paris. After that, it was either kill or be killed. Disappearing might be an option, but he had no idea how far her tentacles could reach.

What was the best ploy? So many options, yet there was only one he kept coming back to: his lies in exchange for her truth.

He said, "You owe me."

Boudica snorted. "I'm sorry, what?"

"You owe me the truth."

She signaled, changed lanes, and turned the radio down. Good. The John Tesh tune was annoying anyway. "I don't owe you shit, Quirk, but I'm curious, so what truth are you talking about?"

"Two years ago, you started recruiting the six of us to be your…army."

"Right."

"Why us? Why this group of people who have such an obscure issue in common?"

"Is this some come-to-Jesus thing where you're having second thoughts? Because I'd say it's a bit late for that now, don't you think?"

"No, I'm curious. Why did you focus on getting

people who had lost somebody the way we did?"

"You want to know the actual truth?"

"That's why I'm asking."

"I read an article about it."

"That's it?"

"Here's the funny thing: Sara Winthrop has been working for LightPulse Productions for decades—have you heard of them?"

"Yeah, they make *Juggernaut*."

"Right. So about two years ago, I'm running a job in Portland for this Somali warlord who wanted this deserter dead and buried. I'm sitting in this bar, having a drink, and in walks Sara Winthrop. I hadn't seen her since high school, but I knew exactly who she was. It brought up a lot of old memories that I'd buried but hadn't forgotten about." Quirk watched as she grew quiet for a moment, staring ahead at the rainy highway but seeing something in her mind. She continued, "I mean, I sat there and I seethed, you know? Like I could've gotten up, walked across the room, and stabbed her in the neck with a fucking fork."

"Obviously you didn't."

"I didn't. I had other work, but I knew I could be patient. The crazy thing was, I was stuck in Portland for about a week, and she kept popping up everywhere. Different magazines, the newspaper—it was like the universe was shoving her in my face, over and over, and then one day, maybe a month later, there was this article in some gaming magazine—I don't even remember what it was called—but some teenage kid had died in North Carolina and there was this huge trial—"

Quirk cleared his throat. "Brandon's?"

"Yep. The one where they quoted you…"

"And Sara Winthrop. Oh my God, that's why her name sounded so familiar. I remembered her in the news after the kidnapping, but there was something else about her name that I couldn't place."

"You were a former enlisted Marine, you were angry, and you were easy to find. It gave me an idea. You were so pissed off after the trial, and I had this thing with Sara and a few of her high school slutbag friends that I needed to deal with. It didn't take long to figure out that hiding my true objective behind the idea of blowing shit up to attract attention to your cause was the way to go. I came up with the idea in about ten minutes, but it took me weeks to round up people with the skills that I needed who had experienced the same type of loss as you."

"So all these places around the world, everything we've done…"

"Julie, Rebecca, Lucy, Colleen…Sara's here in

Portland, and Melinda is in Paris."

"Why?"

"You got what you want, which is attention for your cause, and I get what I want. Retribution."

"For what?" Quirk held back the lies he'd planned to tell. They could wait. She was opening up on her own.

Boudica took her right hand off of the steering wheel and placed it on his thigh. "Remember earlier how I was talking about getting caught?" She smiled and slid her palm farther up his leg, closer to his crotch.

Quirk felt himself stir, despite the situation. "Um, yeah."

"Well," she said, cupping the bulge, gently squeezing, "it's amazing how the mind works, isn't it? How it can take a traumatic experience from our childhood and turn it into a fetish or an insatiable desire? Like how a young girl can be sexually abused and then become a porn star because she still has the daddy issues to work out." She caressed him, softly sliding her hand up and down.

Quirk tried to make the erection disappear. He thought about knitting, baseball, and spoiled milk, anything to take his mind off of it.

Her voice was smooth. Seductive. Quirk imagined

her crawling across the living room floor like a lioness stalking her prey. "They caught me doing something I wasn't supposed to be doing in a place I wasn't supposed to do it. Granted, I *like* being caught now, whether it's sex on a park bench or shoplifting a pack of gum, because that element of danger is so…*exciting*…but back then—"

She squeezed his testicles, hard, and Quirk yelped as the pain coursed into his abdomen. He grew nauseated and doubled over, moaning until she let go.

Boudica said, "Do you feel that, Quirk? Do you feel that pain that's so deep, so intense that you want to vomit just to get it outside your body?"

"Yes," he said, his voice weak and croaking.

Boudica reached under the front seat and removed a small .38 caliber revolver.

The ache in his stomach was so intense he didn't flinch when she rested the barrel against his temple.

"That's the pain they caused me that day and I spent years—*years*—trying to overcome it, but you know what? Some scars never fade. So you think I owe you the truth, Quirk? I *owe* you? Here's your truth, you pathetic bastard: I'm going to end this with or without you, and you can either join me and avenge your little rat nephew, or you can eat a bullet and spare me the indignation because I've got better shit to do."

He coughed, sputtered, and watched the trail of saliva dangling from his bottom lip. He'd intended to lie to her, to tell her that if she killed him, then he had a failsafe plan that would execute if he didn't check in—an anonymous note sent to the FBI, CIA, NSA, and every newspaper editor he could find. Would it have worked? He didn't know. Now he wasn't so sure that she'd care. She'd probably enjoy the notoriety—the potential of being caught.

"You're just going to kill me when you're done. Why should I bother?"

She laughed and shoved the .38 harder against his skull. "I could, yeah, but think about it, moron. Would I have given all that money to you for the other jobs if I were just going to end you when everything's done? What a waste that would've been. If I were going to kill you, I would've done it after Moscow, but then I'd have to start recruiting all over again. It's hard to find good help, so as long as you stick close and do what you're told for as long as I feel like telling you, then don't worry about it. Your skills for your life—how's that sound?"

"Good," he mumbled, though he didn't mean it. He'd be a free prisoner.

"I thought so. Here's the deal, Captain Quirk: we finish up with Portland and Paris, and then we take a nice, long vacation, just the two of us. Maybe you and I will go down to the South Pacific to some small island where nobody cares as long as the tourists spend their money. We'll get some sun and make love wherever we want. It'll be good to get away. After that we come back, we see about getting Shelley Sergeant some time outside, and then we work on making the real money. We have the proper talents, and I know people who need them."

Quirk's abdomen throbbed in pain, but through the hazy fog of ache deep in his belly, he was certain he'd heard her correctly. He knew Boudica was off, but had she just offered to take him somewhere in the South Pacific and relax like two honeymooners? Thirty seconds ago she'd been threatening to put a bullet in his head.

'Insane' didn't grasp the intensity of her emotional instability.

Did he have a choice?

"Sounds awesome," he said, finally able to sit up and take a normal breath.

"I thought it would. And I'm sorry I hurt you. Maybe after we're done with Sara tonight, I'll kiss it and make it better." She smiled and winked.

God help me, Quirk thought.

***

When they were only a couple of miles away from Portland proper, Boudica's cell rang. She answered with a sharp, "What's taking you so long?"

Quirk listened. Whatever had happened didn't sound like it was going according to plan.

She slapped the phone closed and slung it into the cup holder. "Damn it."

He'd decided to play along for the time being. Whether he was temporarily a free prisoner or a soon-to-be South Pacific sex slave to this insane terrorist, being alive and having hope was better than being six feet under. All he had to do was bide his time until the opportunity presented itself. It didn't matter if it happened in two hours, two months, or two years. Life awaited beyond Boudica's grasp, as long as he managed to *stay* alive.

"Who screwed up?" he asked.

"Tank thinks he's made. Sara left with that Sam Elliot-wannabe detective and her children. He thinks they were headed toward Jim Rutherford's house but they've been driving in circles for fifteen minutes."

"Who's Jim Rutherford?"

"Rich bastard that owns LightPulse. Sara's boss."

"Is there anything you *don't* know about her?"

"Nope."

"So if Tank thinks he's made, now what?"

"Maybe I could think of something if you'd shut up."

"If she's with a detective, won't he eventually take her back to the police station?"

"Possibly, but if they were going toward Rutherford's house to begin with, then they must've thought the station was a bad plan."

Quirk suggested, "What if we catch up with him and switch off? He drops the tail and we pick it up. If they think they've pegged him as a tail, it'll confuse the shit out of them if he just pulls into a grocery store parking lot like nothing happened, right? Or they'll think he backed off to recoup and they have an opening. So he'll duck away, we slip in while they're trying to figure out what in the hell happened, and then follow them to wherever they're going. Most likely they'll be suspicious that they're being watched, so if I were them and I thought my tail was gone, I'd get to where I was going as quick as I could."

"That actually makes sense, Quirk. Maybe you're not just a pulse with an erection like I thought."

"Thanks, I think."

She called Tank and explained the plan. She listened, then replied, "Good, I know the road. We'll be there in five minutes, tops. Call back if they change course." Boudica hung up then began dialing again. "Does your house have an alarm?"

"Yeah, but—"

"Is it armed?"

"No, we left too quickly earlier; I didn't have a chance."

"Perfect. We need to get the Spirit or Dimitri over there right now—come on, damn you, pick up—you said the laptop's ready, right?"

"It is, but we'll have to—"

Boudica held up her index finger. "Spirit? What took you so long? Right. Change of plans."

TWENTY-ONE

Barker continued his not-so-subtle evasive driving from street to street, checking his mirrors with each turn. The kids had gotten impatient in the backseat. Jacob was close to peeing in his pants, the girls were complaining about being hungry, and Miss Willow had run out of ideas to keep them occupied.

Sara's hands shook. She had explained the situation to Barker, describing how the two unfamiliar men had been pretending like they weren't staring at her. He wanted her to see if she could get a look at the man driving the Dodge Ram, but every time he slowed down, hoping the truck would get closer, the guy backed off.

Barker had tried so many times to give Sara the chance that they'd wasted close to twenty minutes.

Twenty minutes during which Barker could've radioed for a patrol car to pull the truck over so they could make their escape. She'd suggested, but he'd resisted.

They sat at a traffic light, waiting for it to change.

"I know it's not the wisest choice," he said, "but if they know anything about you at all, they'll know which direction you were headed, especially since our tail saw us pass Rutherford's street. If we call it in and the guy gets pulled over for no reason, they'll for sure know we're onto them and they might have somebody staking out his house before we get there. They could ambush us the second we tried to get inside."

"I suppose. But who's to say he didn't call and tell them where we were headed already?"

"You've got a point, though I think we're safer knowing where he is, at least until we can figure out what to do next."

"I still think we should go to Jim's. I'll call him and tell him to open a garage door for us. We haul ass back there and get inside."

Barker flicked his eyes up to the mirror then nodded. "Okay. We'll hole up and alert the cavalry."

When the light changed from red to green, they inched forward. As Sara pulled her cell from a pocket, Barker reached over and touched her arm. "Hold up."

"Why?"

"He just pulled into McDonald's."

"What?" Sara craned her neck to see over her seat. The pickup cruised out of sight, behind the yellow, red, and beige brick building with the golden arches.

"Yep, he broke off."

"Weird," she said. "You don't think it was just some random guy going our direction, do you?"

"I doubt it. Something's up."

"Then all the more reason to get over to Jim's. Kids, Willow? You guys okay?" She nodded at the chorus of three no's and one gentle smile. "We'll be at Uncle Jim's house soon, I promise."

Barker said, "Looks like he's parking, but it's too far away for me to see who it is. You?"

"I can't tell either. Do you really think he was following us? Why would he give up like that?"

"Honestly, I'm—I don't know. Could be pulling a swap if he thinks he's made."

"Do they do that?"

"'They?'"

"Criminals. Bad guys."

"Probably, but I'm not sticking around to find out. You call Rutherford and let him know we're pulling a stunt-driver move up into that fancy garage of his."

"On it."

While Sara called to let Jim know they were on their way, Barker strained to see if anyone within the traffic behind them changed lanes when he did. While they were on a main road with bumper-to-bumper cars and rain blurring the rear window, it was nearly impossible to tell.

He turned right, heading west, back in the direction of the senior Rutherford's mansion, which wasn't too far from Teddy's place. Barker recalled standing in front of the smaller home—and it seemed funny to think of it as smaller, given its size—along with JonJon, trying to figure out what in the hell was going on with Sara Winthrop's case. DJ, dead and gone. Too soon.

His current partner, another greenhorn named Elkins, was currently on his honeymoon in Jamaica. Good guy, but no more sense than God gave a goose. Maybe he was trainable, but the jury was still out.

Barker glanced behind them. Three cars had made the same turn.

Three was three too many, but they would be easily weeded out with some random direction changes.

Sara hung up. "Jim's ready for us. Says he's got the door to the panic room open as well, in case we need to dash inside."

"I'm hoping it won't be necessary. But we do have some bogeys on our tail. I know it's a long shot, but do you recognize any of those cars behind us? Anybody that might be going Jim's way?"

Sara looked. "Nope. I see a red Jeep Cherokee, some sort of gray crossover model, and…a blue sedan. Oh, the Jeep just turned off."

"Gotcha. One down." Barker turned right down a

side street, then made a left, then another quick left, heading back toward the road they were on. When he stopped at the intersection, the gray crossover vehicle and the blue sedan drove past. A middle-aged blonde woman was driving the crossover, and a woman and a younger man cruised by in the sedan. No one made eye contact through the windows, no one slowed to inspect them, and no one stopped to wait.

Barker grunted a curious, "Hmm."

"Are we clear?"

"Looks like it. I thought for sure they would've traded off if the Ram thought he was made."

"Or maybe he wasn't following us to begin with."

Barker shook his head. "I don't like it. Something's off, but we're closer to Jim's than we are to the station—"

"Barker, forget that you have a badge and a gun for just one minute, please? Now that our home is a big pile of scrap, everything I have is right here in this car with me, okay? Get us to Jim's, we'll camp out in his panic room, and then you can get back out there and start being a cop again. But right now all I want is to be out of the open and in a secure place."

Barker studied her then relented. "Okay."

"Okay?"

"Yeah. I get you. Sometimes it's hard to let go of

the intuition." Barker turned onto Lawson Avenue, and then drove cautiously down the street. The crossover SUV was nowhere to be seen, and the blue sedan had disappeared as well.

When they reached Bellingham, he hesitated before making the turn, counted to three, and said, "Miss Willow, you hold on to those kids back there. This might get bumpy." He jerked the steering wheel to the left and jammed his foot down on the gas pedal. The engine roared. He caught a glimpse of Sara reaching for the handle above the door. In the backseat Jacob cheered, the twins laughed, and Miss Willow closed her eyes.

If The Clan was waiting on them and were prepped for an ambush, then they'd better have a tank or RPG launcher ready to stop the car. Short of a bullet to the head, he was getting Sara's family inside Jim Rutherford's home no matter what gauntlet they had to blaze through.

Parked cars zipped past in a blur of colors, shapes, and sizes.

He checked the speedometer. Fifty in a twenty-five. Not smart, not smart at all, but as long as one of the neighbors didn't decide to back into their path without looking, they'd be fine. He was confident behind the wheel, even on wet blacktop and narrow streets. Too many years of defensive driving classes, too many high-speed chases, gave him the necessary skills to hurtle down the crowded street untouched like a running back through a defensive line, dodging and evading contact.

Sara said, "Barker? Maybe not so fast?"

"We're fine."

"Yeah, but—"

"Relax, Sara. We're almost there and I'm not going to risk giving them a chance—"

Sara's scream was shrill, terrified. "Watch out!"

Barker glanced to the left, catching a fleeting glimpse of a blue car launching at them perpendicularly from a driveway. In that moment time slowed, creeping ahead frame by frame.

Snapshot. Car. Snapshot. Car.

It wasn't unintentional. It wasn't some distracted person backing out of their driveway. The car faced forward, launching straight at them. When his brain registered the intent, the scene before him broke through the slow-motion slideshow and sped up, barely allowing him time to react.

Barker slammed on the brakes and yanked the steering wheel sideways, angling it so that his left front quarter panel intercepted the blue sedan, reducing the brunt force.

A deafening *thud* shook the car, followed by the sounds of crunching, twisting metal. Barker's teeth knocked together as he was pitched to the left, slamming his head against the windshield. It cracked, dazing him, but he blinked, shook his head, and regained control.

Whether it was faulty engineering or a miracle of circumstance, the airbags didn't deploy, granting him continued visibility through the spider web of cracks in the front windshield.

The force of the collision drove his car to the right and they caromed off of a parked Suburban. Metal screeching. Sparks flying. Side-view mirrors ripped from doors.

Sara's children screamed in the backseat.

She turned around and shouted, asking if they were okay, were they hurt, as Barker fought the steering wheel, forcing it to the left, shoving the blue sedan away, but only for an instant.

They made another run at him.

Barker jammed on the brakes and yanked the steering wheel to the right, maneuvering between two cars, across a driveway, and into a yard. He narrowly avoided a small sapling, but a white statue of an angel exploded on impact.

He flashed a look to his left and saw that the blue

sedan had a flat tire, likely from careening into one of the parked cars when he'd darted up into the yard.

Sparks flew from the rim.

"The hedge!" Sara shouted.

It was thick with tangled branches and Barker only had a second to react. Were the branches weak enough for them to barrel through? Doubtful. The bushes were tall with thick trunks. Maybe they could make it through. Maybe not.

Their left side was blocked by a white gazebo and a row of cars parked on the street.

Barker said, "Hold on, we're going through."

The yard dipped slightly down and then angled up again. Barker's sedan bounced, launched, and once airborne, it blasted through the thinner middle of the hedgerow. Leaves and branches flew as they erupted through to the other side. The car landed, slid sideways, and spun in a wide circle, digging up the yard and sending grass and mud scattering.

Barker regained control and aimed for an opening between two trees.

The blue sedan had shot past them and Barker saw an opportunity. He guided his car through the two oaks, slipping to the side and clipping the rear slightly, then felt the tires grab once they were back on the street. Brake lights flashed on the attacking car.

Barker dipped to the right, cut left, and used his left front to nudge just behind their right rear wheel, a perfectly executed PIT maneuver. The blue sedan spun around, slammed against a parked utility truck, and came to a stop.

Sara whipped around. "They're getting out."

"Good. Let 'em stay right there for a bit."

"How is everybody?" Sara asked, looking at Lacey and Callie's terrified faces. Jacob was silent, but seemed to be on the verge of a smile. Boys. Crazy car chases. If he only knew.

Lacey and Callie said they were okay. Miss Willow patted her chest above her heart and agreed.

"Almost there." She turned to Barker. "Should I call 9-1-1?"

"Let's get you guys in the house first; chances are somebody's already beat you to it."

"Right."

Barker turned into Jim Rutherford's short driveway. It angled uphill to a large, brick home with green vines and black shutters. Four tall, white columns stood regally on the front porch, accentuating the black shingles overhead. The massive three-car garage, roughly the size of Barker's home, adjoined the right side, and the far left garage door was open. Jim's forest-green Lexus had been removed and now sat off to the side, leaving the space available.

Barker expected to see Jim standing there waiting on them, but the LightPulse CEO was absent. Was it worth being concerned over? Doubtful. He'd probably seen or heard the commotion down the street and gone inside to report it.

They squeezed through the open garage door and parked. Barker got out, risked a look down the street toward the blue sedan, and saw the two attackers running up the sidewalk. Phone in hand, he backed away, dialing 9-1-1. "Detective Barker here. Get a team to 18972 Bellingham. Rutherford residence. I got two that're possibly armed. They're on foot and in pursuit of an officer and a family. One male, one female. I'll call back when we're secure."

He slapped the garage door button and heard the loud, groaning gears as the door rumbled down the tracks.

Sara, Miss Willow, and the children were standing by the entrance.

"In, now!" Barker said as he ran toward them. "Find Jim and get to the panic room."

TWENTY-TWO

Teddy sat impatiently in the backseat. Up ahead, Bellingham Avenue was awash in a sea of flashing lights and emergency vehicles. Police, fire, and ambulance, they all had the road blocked. To his right, the line of parked cars were scraped and battered, and a few houses down he could see yards that had been damaged and a hedgerow with a gaping hole.

Karen was too close to the car in front of them. The one behind had already nudged the bumper accidentally. They were blocked in and couldn't turn yet, not until their car crept forward to the point where an officer was directing drivers to turn around.

Teddy said, "What happened, Karen? You think my dad's okay?"

"I don't know, Teddy."

To Teddy's left, Dimitri shifted uncomfortably in his seat. He held a silver laptop case close to his chest. He hadn't spoken a word since they'd picked him up outside of a small, one-story house on the east side of the river. He smelled like bad aftershave and cigarettes.

In front of Teddy in the passenger's seat, the Spirit chewed on a coffee straw and appeared lost in thought. He hadn't said much either, and Teddy suspected that in his profession the less said, the better. Karen had insisted on the seating arrangement for safety. Easier to keep an eye on the potential trouble that either of the Russians could cause.

Back in the café, Vadim Bariskov had made them a deal once he'd finished discussing the plans with Boudica. A deal that Teddy didn't like, not in the slightest, but if they wanted Bariskov's help, it was the only available option.

Ivan was a friend.

Sara was the closest thing he had to a sister.

It was an easy decision. She'd saved his life once before. Time to return the favor.

Teddy tapped Bariskov's shoulder as the car inched closer to the patrolman. "Aren't you scared they'll recognize you?" he asked.

"The Spirit, dear boy, is just that…a spirit. Elusive and invisible. Dimitri, on the other hand…"

Dimitri squirmed and took his hand off the laptop case long enough to nervously push his glasses higher on his nose.

Bariskov laughed. "Don't worry, Dimitri! I'll make sure you have only the best boyfriend in prison. I know people."

Dimitri's knee bounced.

Teddy sat back in his seat, slightly worried, but not

officially panicked yet. They were a full block from his father's home, and he prayed that whatever had happened here wasn't a result of anything regarding Sara, or Boudica, or this insane mess.

According to Bariskov, the call from Boudica had provided a short set of instructions. Meet Dimitri at the house, pick him up, and deliver the suitcase to an address that Bariskov wouldn't reveal.

Neither Teddy nor Karen had realized where they were ultimately headed until Bariskov had pointed them down Bellingham. Teddy had protested, but Bariskov assured him that their role was limited and that he would take care of the rest. "We are only delivering this laptop," he'd said. "It has the best surveillance software. Nothing more."

Now, twenty minutes later, Teddy still didn't understand Bariskov's motivations. Every time he'd tried to ask, he'd gotten an evasive answer. Karen wasn't helping. Either she trusted the old Russian, or she was cautiously waiting to see what happened before she made a move. He had to do something. He didn't like this. Not at all.

Teddy said, "Hey, Vadim?"

"What?"

Teddy took a deep breath and pressed forward. "What's the laptop for?"

"*Again* you ask me this?"

"It's a simple question, and I can get you close to Ivan, remember?"

"Fine, fine. Dimitri can use it to access your father's security system. We transmit the signal to Boudica and she gets to keep an eye on your friend Sara if she's there with your father."

"What if she's not?"

"Then we wait."

"Honestly? That's it?"

"True story."

"You spy on my dad's house for a while, just long enough for you to help us get Boudica?"

"I think so, yes."

"You think so? Look, man, we had a deal. You help with Boudica, I get you access to Ivan. There's no 'think so' about it."

"*Teddy*," Karen said.

"What, Karen? I mean, come on, we're sitting in a goddamn car with two international criminals, about to go through a road check, and we're carrying some kind of super spy computer. I'd like to make sure this is worth it before Dimitri and I are stuck in a prison love triangle."

A bead of sweat ran down the side of Dimitri's face.

"I agree with you, but right now we need to stay calm. We don't want to look suspicious, do we? We turn around, take a couple of side streets, and we're back on track. We'll go around and come in from the west side."

"Ah…" Bariskov shook his head. "Not from what I can see. The road is blocked on the other side now, as well."

Teddy leaned up and tried to see around Bariskov's head. "What?"

Karen said to Teddy, "Is he serious?"

"Yeah, looks like it. Oh my God."

"What?"

"It looks like there are some S.W.A.T. guys sneaking up the street. Yeah, they are and they're…oh Jesus, that's my dad's house. They're in front of my dad's house."

"Are you sure?"

"Positive." Teddy lunged and wrapped an arm around Bariskov's neck and pulled him hard back into the seat. "What's happening down there?"

Bariskov sputtered and tried to pull Teddy's arm away. "I don't know," he said. "Dimitri!"

Teddy whipped his head around and stared at Dimitri, waiting on him to fight for Bariskov. Dimitri grinned and looked away.

Teddy squeezed tighter. "Tell me!"

"I don't… I can't breathe."

"Tell me!"

Nervous, looking at the officer then back at Teddy, Karen said, "You two may want to hurry."

Bariskov said, "Okay, okay. Let me breathe and I'll tell you."

Teddy grunted, gave one final squeeze, and then sat back in his seat.

"I told you, this Boudica, she's like a hammer. No style or finesse. Just punch, punch, punch, and she's impatient. Not smart."

Karen rolled down her window and smiled. "Good afternoon, Officer. What's going on down there?"

Teddy winced. What was she doing? Do not engage!

"Ma'am, please pull into this driveway behind me and find an alternate route."

"Can't we get through, just a little ways? We're right down there, at the big brick house with white columns. We're late for a meeting with Mr. Rutherford. He's expecting us."

"I'm afraid that won't be possible, ma'am. Please turn around."

"Okay, but can we get in from the other side?"

"The best I can tell you is to come back later. I'm sure he'll understand. Keep it moving, please, thank you."

Karen smiled and rolled up her window, turned the car around, and headed east on Bellingham, away from Jim Rutherford's home.

Teddy said, "What in the hell are you doing?"

"Getting his attention off of you two idiots."

"Whatever." Teddy said to Bariskov, "You weren't finished."

Bariskov smoothed down his white hair and rubbed his throat. "This hammer, she's erratic. Makes stupid decisions. I don't know how she's survived this long, but there are plenty of people who trust her, who give her money to do jobs for them."

"Then why do you work for her?"

"I told you, she pays big money."

"What happened up there, huh? What's going on at my dad's house?"

Bariskov sighed. "Teddy, Teddy, Teddy, if I knew, I would tell you. She saw an opportunity, she took it, and now, who knows? I'm just surprised she would move forward without the bomb."

"Bomb? What bomb?"

"The one in Dimitri's lap."

"Oh Jesus." Teddy pushed himself away from

Dimitri as far as he could get. "That's a bomb?"

"Yes, a very powerful one, so I would not make Dimitri angry if I were you."

Dimitri winked and finally spoke. "Relax. It's very stable."

Karen said to Bariskov, "You son of a bitch."

Teddy added, "You *lying* son of a bitch."

"If I would've told you what was in there, you would've tried to stop us, and I would've had to kill you, see? This way you stay alive, you give me Ivan. All good thoughts in the Spirit's head. I think things through."

"Are you serious? How's it a good thing that you were going to blow up my father?"

"Not the plan. Well, not exactly."

"Then what was?"

"Boudica, she wanted us to bring the bomb while Sara Winthrop was trapped in your father's house. We bring the bomb, she blows up the house, game over. But, as you can see, something happened. She changed her mind; who can say why? Now we do it differently."

"Forget it. We're done here."

Karen pulled into the parking lot of an empty building. The drive-through window configuration suggested it used to be a bank. "Teddy," she said. "Try your dad. Try Sara. Maybe they're out. We don't know what's going on."

"Yeah, good idea." He fished his cell from his pocket and dialed. "No answer on Sara's cell." He hung up and dialed again. "Nothing on my dad's, either."

"Try his home number."

Teddy dialed and waited. He watched Karen in the mirror. They made eye contact and hope passed between their gaze.

A woman answered. "Is this the White Knight riding in on his horse?"

Teddy mouthed, "I think it's her."

Karen whispered, "Be careful."

"Who is this?" he asked.

"Introductions aren't necessary, Teddy. You know who I am."

"Where's my dad? Where's Sara?"

"Oh, we're all enjoying a game of Monopoly in the living room."

Teddy couldn't contain himself. "You let them go," he shouted.

The amusement was audible in her voice. "Has that ever worked in the history of hostages?"

He tried a different tactic. "What do you want?"

"Nothing, Teddy. I have everything I need right here." Teddy listened to what sounded like a yelp from

Sara, and then heard his father telling him to stay away and let the police handle it. "Now, now, Jim, you know that won't work. Teddy?"

"What?"

"I had to threaten little Jacob with a bullet to get this out of him, but Daddy Dearest tells me there's a secret entrance one street over. He suggested we could leave his house that way, but I don't think I'm ready for that just yet. And besides, I got quite an interesting message from a contact of mine earlier. Let me speak to the Spirit."

Teddy handed his cell phone over the seat. "She wants to talk to you."

Bariskov looked surprised, but took the phone, cleared his throat, and said, "They were looking for *you*, but they found me instead. Do not worry, I have it under control."

Teddy and Karen exchanged glances. Dimitri tapped his foot.

Bariskov nodded. "Yes, Dimitri has it… No. No way. You've looked outside the window, haven't you? They're everywhere… And he knows where it is? Okay, give us a few minutes." Bariskov ended the call and said to Teddy, "She wants us to bring the bomb inside using your father's secret entrance."

Karen asked, "What secret entrance?"

"It's over on Elgin, one street behind my dad's place."

"He never told me about that."

"Why would he?"

"What's it for?"

"He's a rich billionaire with too many obsessive ideas. If he's paranoid enough to have a panic room, he's paranoid enough to have a way out of the house that doesn't involve the front or back doors."

"But why?"

"Can we not discuss this in front of Boris and Natasha, please?" In truth, Jim had spent a tremendous amount of money five years ago to have the escape route installed, involving numerous "donations" that weren't quite bribes, along with highly visible public support of Portland's new mayor. Jim had been convinced that with the astounding success of *Juggernaut* the threats of corporate espionage would increase and there was the potential for an attempt on his life.

Teddy had scoffed at the time and insisted his father had been reading too many Grisham novels, but after the insanity with Shelley Sergeant, however unrelated it may have been, well, now it seemed justifiable.

Karen nodded. "Fine. Then what's the plan, Bariskov?"

"Why're you asking him?"

"Forgive me if I ask the international criminal who's been doing this for fifty years what the best options are. Now, do you mind?"

Teddy said, "Go ahead," then glanced at Dimitri and rolled his eyes.

Dimitri chuckled his agreement.

Bariskov said to Karen, "Easy as cake. No…pie? Easy as pie? Teddy and I will go in this escape route. *Pop, pop*, Boudica is done, Teddy takes the credit, and I disappear. We'll discuss Ivan later, yes?"

"What about Dimitri?"

"He'll survive on his own. Unless, of course, Miss Wallace wants him dead. Eh, Dimitri? You'll behave?"

Dimitri nodded.

"Good," said Bariskov. "Teddy, bring the bomb. She'll be suspicious if we show up without it."

"I'm not touching that thing," he said, yet he knew he had to for his dad's sake, for the children, for Willow, and for Sara.

Dig deep, Teddy. Time to man up again.

TWENTY-THREE

Sara and Barker sat on Jim Rutherford's living room floor with their backs against a low, white wall. Behind them, stairs led down to a lower level with a small movie theater and extra bedrooms. Beyond that was another set of stairs leading to the basement.

Lacey, Callie, and Jacob, along with Miss Willow, were sequestered in the game room down the hallway where one of Patty Kellog's goons watched over them.

Jim Rutherford had been tied up and silenced with a strip of duct tape across his mouth. He sat in a chair in front of the fireplace, glasses missing, shirt ripped, with his nose bleeding and a dark bruise under his left eye.

The phrase, "Like father, like son," ran through Sara's mind as she watched him struggle to breathe while he drifted in and out of consciousness. Not too long ago, Teddy had been in that same position, trapped in the abandoned cabin to the east of Portland. Sara wondered where Karen and Teddy were. Had they found Vadim Bariskov, and would they be able to help if they had? Given the preparedness of The Clan, truthfully she expected them to be discovered floating facedown in the Willamette a few days from now.

Earlier, as they'd burst through the door leading from Jim's garage and into the massive kitchen, they'd only made it to the hallway entrance before Sara heard Barker yelp followed by a loud *thump*, and then another as he'd fallen to the floor. Sara had turned and saw a younger man holding what looked like a fully automatic weapon.

The guy was one of the two men that had been staring at her outside her home.

He had nudged Barker's ribs to make sure he was out then ordered Sara, Miss Willow, and the kids into the living room.

Thirty seconds later, a woman who had to be Patty Kellog and a younger, timid guy whom she referred to as "Quirk" had arrived through the front door, and then, two minutes after that, as Sara and her family sat on the couch, huddled together and fearful, another man had burst into the home. Sara had recognized him, too. Earlier he'd been staring at her with his partner. Was he the one driving the Dodge Ram?

Patty *resembled* the girl Sara remembered from twenty years ago, but she'd had some plastic surgery done. Higher cheekbones, a thinner nose. She'd lost weight and changed the color of her hair. Regardless, it was her. Different, but the same.

Now, Patty, Quirk, and the one they called Rocket stood with their backs to the wall, occasionally pulling at the curtains to survey the growing commotion outside. From the game room, the guy they called Tank yelled, "Three more commandos just took up spots behind that black Toyota."

"Got 'em," Rocket called back.

"I don't see any snipers yet, but that doesn't mean they aren't there."

"Roger that."

Sara said, "Patty, I think—"

"I don't care what you think." Patty moved away from the window, across the massive expanse of the living room, and stepped around the overturned couch and coffee table. She tucked her handgun into her waistband and slapped Sara hard across the cheek.

Barker and Sara were bound just like Jim, wrists and ankles cinched tightly together. Barker shouted, "That's enough!" and got a hard backhand to his jaw.

Patty shook her hand and flexed it.

Barker spat a mouthful of blood onto the white carpet.

Patty squatted low in front of Sara and shoved a finger into her face. "As soon as the Spirit gets here with the bomb…" She made an explosion noise, and then spread her arms overhead in a large arc. "We're gone and you're done. After that there's only one more of you bitches to take care of, and I hear Paris is great this time of year."

Sara shook her head. "I'm sorry, Patty. Oh my God, I am so sorry, but you can't blow up the memories."

Patty slapped Sara again.

Barker tried to lunge for her. Patty was faster. He halted with the handgun barrel against the center of his forehead. Patty clenched her teeth. "One more time. Try it. Give me a reason."

Barker sat back, fuming.

Sara tried again. "I know what they did was wrong—"

"They? They? You were *there*, Sara. You watched and did nothing. You *did* nothing, you *said* nothing, and then you had the nerve to look me in the eye when we passed each other in the hall until they took me away. Look at these. Look!" Patty showed her the scars on her wrists. "Too bad for you it didn't work, huh?"

"I'm sorry," Sara said. "That's all I can say. We were sixteen. It's been so long."

"You know what's neat about this situation, Sara? I don't really give a good goddamn what's going on outside. Let them bring in the S.W.A.T. team or whoever; I don't give a shit, because you know what's so great about it? Julie, Rebecca, Lucy, and Colleen all died without me being able to see their faces before it happened. That's my one regret. I didn't think it through. I thought as long as they got what they deserved, it was fine. But no, oh no, this is *so* much better. Watching you beg, waiting for the end to come. God, this is infinitely more satisfying and if I'd known—man, if I'd known—I would've done it so much differently with the other four. And believe me, Melinda is going to have it a lot worse than you, because now I know to drag it out and relish every...single...moment."

Jim groaned and opened his eyes. He mumbled something and then passed out once more.

Quirk, from his position by the massive picture window, said, "It looks like they want to talk. They're sending some guy up the sidewalk with a megaphone."

"Ignore them. We wait."

"But what if we—"

Patty shouted, "Quirk, do you want to make it out of here alive?"

He nodded, swallowing so hard that Sara could see him do it from across the room.

"Then shut up and trust me."

"Okay." He closed his eyes and leaned his head back against the wall.

From outside, they all heard the magnified voice of a man asking to speak to a representative.

Patty said to Sara, "You know, if you think about it, this is perfect justice. We've been doing this under the guise of a guerrilla group, trying to draw attention to the sad, sad plight of video game violence. Trust me, I have some sympathy for the poor people it happened to, but it's never hit me close to home." She chuckled. "Well, maybe that's because I was too screwed up to have a home and a family, but Quirk, the quivering pansy over there, his nephew took a bullet to the chest. Rocket's little brother tried to shoot a kid with a .22 pistol and when he missed, the target and his buddies beat him to death, all because he beat their high score.

"Tank's sister got obsessed with a game and drank a bottle of bleach when her character died. There are three others in our group—well, two now, since Cleo's gone—that had to deal with something similar. All of them, every single one, was because of *Juggernaut*. Do you have any idea how long it took me to find these people? I mean, really, it's just so damn perfect. I hadn't forgotten about you, not in the slightest, but one day I happened to catch the article about you and Shelley Sergeant. A few bright ideas later and here we are, about to blow up the house of the man responsible for six deaths and his number one accomplice. It's crazy how it all came together. We'll release a statement, the media will eat it up, and we'll be drinking French wine and finishing up with Melinda before they're done sifting through the ashes."

Sara said, "Don't you think they'll have looked at the house plans by now and seen Jim's way out of here? You think you can just sneak out the back door?"

"If they knew about it, they'd be in here already. Jim was smart, weren't you?"

Jim mumbled something and lifted his head.

Patty asked him, "How much did you pay to keep the tunnel plans out of the official records?"

Jim grunted and looked away.

"See, Sara? For all their guns and all their flashing lights, all their training and tactics, their bullets and shouting and plans, what trumps it? Huh? *Money.* Funny thing, isn't it? His money will save our asses while they're picking up pieces of yours."

The lump in Sara's throat felt like a softball as she tried to choke it down. They were done. Her children, Miss Willow, Barker, and Jim. This was it. She'd survived so much over the past four years. She'd been tough. She'd outlasted Brian's disappearance. She'd fought Shelley and won. She'd come so far, and now, all the struggle and perseverance had been for nothing.

She couldn't see another way out. Patty was right. They were dead, but maybe not all of them. "Please," Sara begged. "Can you at least let my children go? They don't deserve this."

Patty glanced down the hallway, and for a moment Sara thought she was considering it. At least until Patty said, "Do the innocent ever deserve anything?"

Rocket said, "Uh, it looks like the FBI's out there now. I see the jackets, the blue ones with the yellow letters."

Patty stood, kicked Sara in the thigh, and backed away. "I'm surprised it took this long. I put a bullet in Agent Timms, what, four or five hours ago? What do you think, Detective Barker? Are Portland's finest and the FBI out there having a pissing contest over jurisdiction?"

Barker ignored her.

"Patty, I'm begging you," Sara said. "Send the kids out, send Barker and Willow and Jim out. This is between you and me."

"No."

"But why? It's my fault. Not theirs."

"It's a simple answer, Sara. I don't *want* to. I *like* watching people suffer. I like being the one in control, unlike that night under the bleachers when I didn't have a fucking choice!"

Behind them, a voice came up the stairway. It was foreign, tainted with what sounded like Russian. "Shouting, shouting, shouting. Always with the shouting, Boudica."

Patty darted around to the top of the stairs. "It's about damn time, Bariskov. What took you—what's he doing here? I thought I told you to kill him once you were in."

Sara tried to see whom Patty was referring to as an aging man in a long brown overcoat stepped into the living room carrying a silver case. He removed his hat and surveyed the madness.

Who followed was a complete surprise, and Sara never thought she'd be so happy to see the annoying, wonderful Teddy Rutherford. She didn't know why. It wasn't like Teddy would be able to do anything other than provide Patty with the encouragement to kill them all faster.

Teddy held his hands up and glanced around the room. When he saw Jim bound to the chair, he shouted, "Dad!" and moved toward him.

Patty aimed her handgun at Teddy's forehead and he froze.

The man she called Bariskov, who had to be the Spirit that Karen had referred to, surveyed the room and scoffed. "Stupid this, stupid that. You behave like a bull, Boudica, stomping through a garden, ruining everything."

"I don't pay you for advice. I pay you to do what I say, when I say it."

Bariskov frowned and shrugged. "Maybe so, but I also like to work with professionals. This—look at this mess, it's the work of an amateur."

Sara wondered what was going on. The power struggle between them seemed foreign, as if Patty hadn't expected it.

Teddy caught Sara's eye. It was brief, barely more than a flicker, but she was certain she saw a wink.

Oh God, Teddy, don't do it, she thought. *You'll get yourself killed.*

But then again, he was here. He didn't seem to be in any direct danger with Bariskov. Did he have a plan? Did *they* have a plan?

Barker must have sensed something, as well. He was subtly working his hands behind his back, trying to loosen the ropes around his wrists.

Bariskov asked, "Did you know they were coming here?"

"Yes," Patty answered.

"Then why didn't you wait?"

"What do you mean?"

"We saw the damage outside, down the street.

Cars ruined, yards ruined, and now look outside—you made this mess. A bull through a garden. So tell me, why not wait? Why not handle it with style and grace?"

Patty shook her head and held out a hand. "We couldn't be sure that Rocket was in place, so I-I saw an opportunity and I took it."

Bariskov shook a finger at her like a parent admonishing a child. "Opportunity does not always create success."

Patty reached for the silver case. "I don't have time for lectures. Just give me the bomb."

Bariskov pulled it away. "Patience, child."

She held out her hand. "Now, Bariskov." Pointing at Teddy, she said, "Rocket, get over here and tie up this dumbass that was stupid enough to walk into a house full of terrorists."

Teddy said, "No thanks, I'm good," as Bariskov threw his hat into Patty's face, distracting her.

Sara held her breath and prayed.

TWENTY-FOUR

Adrenaline pumped through Teddy's veins.

He heard only the sound of his own heartbeat.

Time moved in slowed, measured increments.

Thump-thump. Thump-thump.

He lifted his shirt, reached behind his back and removed the sub-compact 9mm that Bariskov had given him before they entered the tunnel leading to Jim's basement.

Thump-thump. Thump-thump.

He swung the gun to his left, aimed quickly, and—

***

Minutes earlier, Karen had dropped them off in front of a small dog park. She'd told him to be careful and asked them both if they wanted her to wait, then ordered Dimitri into the front seat where she could keep an eye on him.

"I can wait here," she insisted.

"No," Bariskov said. "You might attract attention. Dimitri will tell you where to go. Teddy will be fine with me."

She cursed, shook her head, and drove away.

Teddy had wondered if he'd ever see her again. Even worse, he wondered if he was on a death mission. Did he really have faith in Bariskov?

"Where is this tunnel…secret passage…whatever you call it?"

"There." Teddy pointed at a small brown building with a beige door, dirt-colored shingles, and a single word stenciled on the entrance: "UTILITY."

Bariskov grunted. "One would never know."

"That's the idea, isn't it? When Dad moved into his house, this neighborhood was full of all of these homes for sale because the housing bubble popped and so many people were upside down on their mortgages. There used to be two houses right here, side by side, and he had them torn down and turned into a dog park. I think that's how he got by the city building codes, you know, long enough for the administrative guys to look away."

Bariskov appeared confused. "What kind of secret is protected by machines digging a tunnel? People would see, no?"

"Wasn't an issue. The tunnel ties into the drainage system underneath. If anybody paid attention long enough to notice, they probably thought they were working on the bathrooms over there." He pointed about twenty yards to his right, then back to the falsely identified utility building. "We go in here, follow the drainage tunnels straight west until we get to the spot that cuts over and up into the entrance in my dad's basement. No big deal."

"No big deal, he says." Bariskov grinned, showing his yellow-stained teeth, and then slapped Teddy on the back. "Confident now, but wait until we get inside."

Teddy put his hands on his hips and sighed. "Yeah, about that…"

***

Teddy moved.

Thump-thump. Thump-thump.

Would the plan work? Would it work well enough to create a diversion? Before entering the basement, Bariskov had insisted he could handle Boudica's thugs, but offered Teddy the gun and asked if he knew how to use it. Of course he did, but he hoped it wasn't much different than the shooting range.

The man by the window turned and raised his hands. He appeared to be unarmed.

Teddy couldn't risk lives on appearances. He squeezed the trigger.

The *chuff* from the silencer sounded thick, dull, and

hollow underneath the rhythmic pounding of his pulse. A red splotch appeared where he'd aimed. Was it luck? Was it skill? After so many hours of testing *Juggernaut*'s virtual weapons systems, maybe it was the latter. The guy fell back against the wall.

There was movement to Teddy's right. He pivoted and saw the woman bringing her arm up, handgun extending from it as Bariskov lunged at her.

Behind them, the second man at the window lifted his weapon. Teddy aimed, fired, and dropped him with a bullet to the forehead. Action without thought. Trusted instincts and learned abilities. The body flopped to the side.

Bariskov lowered a shoulder and drove it into the woman's chest. She flew backward, flailing her arms, trying to catch her balance. She tripped over a cushion that had fallen from one of the overturned couches. As she fell her weapon fired, the sound also muffled by a silencer.

Teddy felt something like a sledgehammer slam into his left thigh and he tumbled sideways and dropped to one knee. He screamed. To his right, Detective Barker was pushing himself up from the floor.

The woman fired again. Teddy heard the *chuff* from her silencer again, saw Bariskov spin to the side from impact, and then pitch to his left. Barker, with his ankles still tied together, launched himself awkwardly from a crouch and pounced on her, knocking her gun free. Barker lifted his head and drove it into her mouth.

She screamed and clawed the floor for her weapon. Barker drove another head butt into her temple and she went silent.

Bariskov groaned and lifted a bloody hand from his side, staring at his slick red palm.

"Is that everybody?" Teddy asked.

Barker said, "No, there's one more down the—"

Three more gunshots sounded as stuffing exploded from the couch next to Teddy's shoulder. He dropped, rolled, and looked up, hearing a fourth shot followed by a fifth.

He wondered why the place hadn't been stormed by the law enforcement outside yet. Did they even know what was happening? Every shot fired had been through a silencer. Maybe they'd heard. Maybe they'd seen through the curtains. Maybe they were waiting for the firefight to die down.

Maybe they had no idea.

Teddy rolled behind the overturned coffee table and chanced a peek over the top. The fourth man, a massive brute in a black jacket and black pants, ducked into the living room and then dropped behind the end section of the low wall. Teddy squirmed around so that the gaping mouth of the stairway entrance was in front of him. He fired the remaining rounds of his clip through the thin wall. Plaster exploded and rained down.

Teddy exhaled when he heard the dull *thud* of a body dropping.

To his left, Barker said, "He's down! He's down!"

Teddy's leg throbbed. He managed to crawl around and scramble up to his feet. Nearby, Bariskov kneeled over Sara, untying her while Barker used the ropes to hogtie the woman.

Jim's chair had overturned during the melee. Teddy hobbled over to him and found his father lying on his side, wounded and unable to get free. He'd taken a stray bullet and his shoulder was wet with blood. "Dad, you're okay."

Jim croaked, "Where'd you learn to shoot like that? You're a hero, son."

Teddy shook his head. "No, too many video games."

"Well, tell *that* to the media."

As soon as Bariskov had Sara free, she sprinted down the hallway. Teddy untied Jim, made sure he was strong enough to stand, and then followed Sara.

Limping along, he found her and her children in the game room, crying, smiling, and hugging each other. Miss Willow had her arms wrapped around them all.

Teddy stopped and watched them, smiling. He wanted to join the group hug. The old Teddy would've jumped right in without thought or regard. He gave himself a mental pat on the back for resisting the impulse. His father, Sara, and Dr. Hanks would be impressed. He shifted his weight and felt the dull, throbbing ache in his leg.

Another pat on the back, he thought. *You got shot.* He mumbled, "You're a beast, Teddy."

Sara lifted her head, smiled, and said, "Did you just say that out loud?"

Teddy blinked. "Say what?"

"Did you just call yourself a beast?"

"Uh…no."

"Well, you should; you got shot!" She stood, moved swiftly, and hugged him. "And you saved our lives. I mean, my God, Teddy, that was unreal." Jacob darted over and wrapped his arms around Teddy's good leg and the twins followed. Miss Willow, who'd also never been his biggest fan, even joined them.

Sara added, "Say thanks to Uncle Teddy, kids."

Uncle Teddy. It had a nice ring to it.

***

Teddy heard Barker in the living room, shouting a short, alarmed burst of, "Sara! Teddy!"

"Yeah?" Sara called back.

Barker appeared in the doorway, breathless, both hands on either side of the doorjamb. "We need to go, right now."

"Why?"

He rushed into the game room and picked up Jacob. "No questions. Go, go, go," he said, urging Sara, the girls, and Miss Willow out the door. Looking back at Teddy over his shoulder, he asked, "You good? Can you move fast enough on that leg?"

"I think so. What's happening?"

"Your Russian buddy says the bomb activated and there's only about two minutes left on the timer."

"What? How?"

"Doesn't matter. He can't shut it down and we're moving."

Jim shouted down the hall, "Hurry!"

In the living room Bariskov stood at the head of the stairs, holding his hat in one hand while the other hand covered the wound in his abdomen.

"What're you waiting on?" Teddy said to Bariskov as the others rushed for the front door.

"I can't go out there."

"We have to."

"No, Teddy, I'm a free man, and I'm going to stay that way."

Barker opened the front door and walked out with one hand raised, carrying Jacob. Teddy could hear him saying, "Hostages coming out! Whoa! Whoa! Get back! Get everybody back! There's a bomb—whole place is gonna go. Move, move!"

"Okay," Teddy said to Bariskov. "You know the way out. You're the Spirit, right? You walk through a wall in Portland and show up in Sweden?"

"This is true."

"Then go. And…thank you."

Bariskov slipped his hat onto his head and pulled it low over his eyes. "Don't forget, you still have to honor your end of the deal."

Teddy shook his head. "Ivan's my friend. Giving you a head start down that tunnel makes us even, so do your thing and disappear, Casper."

Bariskov winked. "You'll see me again."

"Let's hope we're on the same side."

Teddy hobbled for the door.

Out in the yard, his father and Barker sprinted over, lifted him off his feet, and carried him, running after the rctreating crowd.

They managed to duck behind an ambulance as the explosion shook the ground.

***

The next day, Sara walked into Room 343 at the hospital and found Teddy sitting up, eating ice cream from a small cup. At his bedside was a beautiful blonde woman she'd never seen before.

Teddy beamed when he saw her. "Sara!"

"Hey there, Beast."

He chuckled and rolled his eyes. "Badass Chick and the Beast. Sounds like a horrible musical."

"So true."

"This is Irina, my…um…she's a friend."

Irina smiled and stood. She shook hands with Sara, and then kissed Teddy on the forehead. "I'll be back later, okay? And my apologies, Sara, my grandfather is ill and I have to get back to Firebrand before the new manager screws something up."

When she was gone, Sara asked Teddy, "Firebrand? Isn't that where you used to go talk to those guys about Red Mob?"

"Yep."

"Wait a second, was she…was that the meth addict that had the hots for you, like, five years ago?"

"Yep."

"And she's here. For you."

"Yep."

"She looks amazing."

"I know, right? And she *wanted* to be here. For me. Can you believe it?"

Sara chuckled and pinched his cheek. "She doesn't know you very well, does she?"

"Hey."

"Joking. Chill, dude. So how're you feeling?"

"Better. These pain meds are amazing."

Sara pulled the chair closer to the bed and sat down. She leaned onto the armrests. "So you want to hear the latest? Or at least what Barker was allowed to tell me?"

"Of course."

"Do you want the good news, the bad news, or the worse news first?"

"The bad news."

"Okay. Your dad's house and everything in it basically evaporated, same as my house. So all your Little League trophies are gone."

"That's not bad news, that's horrible news."

"About the house or the trophies?"

"The trophies!"

"Figures."

"What's the good news?"

"Karen's going to be fine, and they caught that guy Dimitri trying to board a plane in PDX with a fake passport. From what Barker says, the scumbag tried to remotely detonate the bomb to wipe his criminal connections clean. He wanted out of that life entirely. Instead, he's going to prison. Out of the frying pan and into the fire, huh?"

"Jesus. Glad they caught him, but Karen—she's not hurt too badly, is she? What happened?"

"So he knocked Karen out, they ran into the ditch, the guy set the bomb to ticking and thankfully, your comrade Bariskov thought to check it. It's so unbelievable to think we were about ninety seconds away from…away from…"

"*Kaboom*?"

"Yeah."

Teddy set his ice cream down on the rollaway table and pushed the recline button on the bed controls. Sara waited while the gears groaned and lowered him. "You said there's worse news?"

"Uh-huh."

"Do I even want to hear it?" He fluffed the pillows and tried to get comfortable.

Sara stood up and went to the window. She put her hands in her pockets and stared at the world outside. What she was about to say meant more to her, her family, and her life than it did to Teddy, but it was important that he knew.

"Sara? What happened?"

"They could only identify three bodies. They found nothing but parts, mostly."

"Which three?"

"Bariskov wasn't one of them."

"And?"

Sara crossed her arms and walked across the hospital room. "Neither was Patty Kellog. They think she got out somehow."

"Oh God, so she's still out there? What're you gonna do?"

Sara took Teddy's hand in hers and held it tenderly. "I don't know. Run…hide."

"No. We can take her."

"It's the best option, Teddy. Your dad thinks so. Barker thinks so."

"You do what you gotta do, but who's going to keep me in line if you're gone?"

"We'll see you around, I'm sure." Sara bent down and kissed his forehead. "I have to run, okay? I don't feel comfortable having the kids out of my sight for too long."

"See you soon, Sara."

"Thanks for saving our lives. You take care of yourself, Beast."

Teddy smiled.

As Sara left the room, she took one last look at him and thought about how strange it was to be so *proud* of the little bastard.

Author's Note

Dear Reader,

I hope you had fun reading SARA'S PAST! Many independent authors depend on dedicated readers and fans like you to get the word out about their books. If you've enjoyed this novel, please consider leaving a review on the site where you purchased it. (It doesn't have to be much. Even a couple of sentences can help convince another reader to take a chance!)

Be First in Line to Learn About New Releases
Visit ErnieLindsey.com to join the email list.
Please note that the third installment, SARA'S FEAR, will be available soon. Sign up to learn when.

Thanks go out to my editors, beta readers, and friends for their dedication and help with getting my fiction out into the world. Much appreciation goes to Jason Gurley for the amazing cover work; be sure to check out his fiction as well. Additionally, my career as an author would not be possible without the support of my patient and understanding wife, Sarah.

Follow Me on Facebook
www.facebook.com/ErnieLindseyFiction

Lastly, to the readers: without you, none of this would be possible. Your continued support enables these voices to get out of my head and onto the page. If you keep reading, I'll keep writing. I love hearing from you guys so please feel free to get in touch via email or social media.

All best,
Ernie Lindsey
January 2014